A WALK WITH LOVE AND DEATH

A NOVEL BY
HANS KONINGSBERGER

SIMON AND SCHUSTER
New York, 1961

LIBRARY OF CONGRESS CATALOG CARD NUMBER: 61–5839
MANUFACTURED IN THE UNITED STATES OF AMERICA
BY GEORGE MCKIBBIN & SONS, BRATTLEBORO, VT.

A WALK
WITH LOVE
AND
DEATH

I

. . . .

IN THE SPRING OF THAT YEAR, 1358, THE PEASANTS OF
northern France did not sow their fields any more.

I had succeeded in getting out of Paris just before sunset and walked to Saint-Denis in the twilight; I had
found a room there to sleep and now was on the road
again.

The sun was rising almost opposite me; a harsh light
skimmed the empty fields. The war was in its twentieth
year, but I was happy.

Not a soul was to be seen. Birds had been singing at
dawn; now there was silence, and not the silence of nature but of a walled-in room in a castle.

After an hour I came to a well near the roadside. It
was surrounded by ruins, but they were old and friendly
with grass growing over them. The water stood high in
the well and was easy to reach. I installed myself in the
sun on the corner of a crumbling wall and pulled out my
bread.

Then suddenly a shabby man on a horse was standing

3

beside me. Around me the plain lay black and bare and yet I had not seen him approach. I went on eating my bread.

"Are you going to Paris?" he asked.

"No, north."

"On foot?"

I didn't answer.

"You will need a horse," he said, "for there aren't many places left in Ile de France where you can find a room or a meal."

I shrugged and he gave me a smile and went on, "I have no use for this horse in Paris. I'll sell it to you, you can have it for two francs."

Two francs was unbelievably cheap even for his skinny horse, and I had twenty francs in the lining of my jacket.

"If you wonder why I would do such a thing," he added, "it's that I can see you're a student. I admire learning; I would want to be a scholar myself."

It was the bread that saved me. Before reaching for my jacket to bring out the two francs I put the last piece in my mouth, and while I did so I saw that he brought his right hand across his body to the handle of an old sword hanging on his left side, away from me. And without looking up at his face I realized that he would kill me the moment I showed my money.

I went on chewing slowly and then I turned toward him again and said, "You are very generous, but the sad truth is that I haven't got a sou, let alone two francs. For the love of learning, why don't you make a gift of your horse to me?"

His hand came back. "Perhaps walking is good for young men," he said and rode off so sharply that lumps of earth flew into my lap.

After that I went on my way again. It was getting warmer and a light haze was rising from the puddles in the road and in the fields. The landscape was empty once more.

2
. . . .

AROUND NOON I CAME UPON THE BODY OF A DOG LYING IN
the road. Big winter flies rose silently as I walked by it. I
had been wondering what that black spot, shifting
slightly, could be; and for some reason the discovery that
it was a dead dog covered with flies unnerved me completely. What the man on the horse had failed to do, the
dog achieved: it made me realize that I had left the pro-
tective ring of the city but without entering nature, that
I was moving in a deadly no man's land.

I stood still. The road ahead of me suddenly seemed
implacable, the lightheartedness with which I had set
out on my journey now was beyond my understanding.
I had a feeling of being lost and alone on earth, a feeling
such as I'd had before only at night in the hour that pre-
cedes dawn—not under a spring sun.

This is the road of the fourth horseman of the Apoca-
lypse, I said to myself.

And I felt better. For that thought took me back to the

university and to the house in Paris where I had lived and where the Revelation of Saint John was nothing more than a splinter of all things men believed; and with that the world brightened again.

But I jumped the muddy ditch and left that road; I set out at a right angle to it and went across the fields, going northeast.

Still nothing but weeds grew on the black land, and there was still no sign of human life; but after a while I came upon a cluster of trees. I found a sheltered hollow, and covered myself with my jacket and rested some time.

After that the going was harder, for the ground became hilly. Now I saw the first peasant's hut and while I hesitated whether to look for shelter there, I saw another farther on, and then another; and I decided I could try to make a bit more headway. No smoke came from the huts and when I passed one close by I saw that it was uninhabited.

I walked along the foot of a rather steep hillside which faced south, and here the slope was planted with vines. They looked sickly but they were growing in rows. Someone was establishing order, some human being was near. From the corner of my eye I saw a shadow move and I turned: an old man was crouching between the vines. In his left hand he held a bunch of weeds he must have been pulling out, his right hand rested on a stone. He ducked low and peered at me with a frown.

7

"I'm alone," I shouted at him, "unarmed!" I held my hands out and he scrambled to his feet and came toward me.

"Have you money?" he murmured.

"What have you got for sale?"

"I've wine, I've wine," he said.

"No food?"

"No."

"Is there a house anywhere near?"

He pointed east, where the ground fell away slightly from his hill. Far away in the plain a row of beeches was just barely visible, catching the sunrays.

"Is it empty?" I asked.

He grinned.

"Well?"

He didn't answer, but shuffled away. I sat down on a bench, and he came back with a dirty jug which he handed to me.

I wiped the edge and drank; it was without doubt the foulest wine I'd ever tasted. But I drank it all. I gave him back the jug and a coin.

"A captain lives in the house," he then said quite loudly.

"What kind of captain?"

He shrugged.

"Is it safe?"

"You must pay," he said. "But you'll pay on every

8

road—" he moved his hand up and down and let it circle around as if the horizon were a cake he was dividing up. "His men are over there, everywhere."

3
· · · · · · ·

MY PROGRESS TOWARD THAT HOUSE WAS FAST; I THINK I
ran part of the way. But I'm not certain, for with no
food and the wine sloshing around in me, the world
became a dreamlike place. The air grew cold, the low
light of the late afternoon made everything sparkle,
and I flew along.

In the great silence I heard several times the sound
of horses without seeing them, and then I let myself
fall flat on the ground and did not stir. I thought, no
matter who that captain may be, it's a good idea to
walk into his establishment as a guest and not as a
prisoner of one of his patrols. But it was much more a
game with me than deliberation. I lay down and put
my mouth against the icy chunks of the earth which
had been plowed but not sown; I decided earth tasted
good and laughed a bit about that. And I thought,
sleeping is being like a tree, dreaming an animal, being
awake a man, and exaltation is being like God. Perhaps not such a very striking thought, but striking

enough to get kicked out of the university for, as I know.

I liked that hour, I liked my fast journey with a hard evening wind and the setting sun pushing in my back. And then I was at the row of beeches and my exaltation ebbed away although I tried to hold on to it. I was no longer alone, there was a house, voices, steps. I was so tired now that I could hardly draw breath. Opposite me the thin slice of the new moon was visible in the sky. It would be a dark night.

I brushed the earth off my clothes and then marched out from behind the trees and toward the door without looking sideways where I heard men talking.

The captain or what looked like a captain was sitting behind a table, leaning on it with his elbows; a heavy-set soldier, eating and drinking with both hands. He could be an army officer or the headman of a Free Company, which is a euphemism for a gang of bandits. He could be fighting for the English, for Navarre, or just for himself, he could be from anywhere and for anyone; perhaps he didn't even know any more. It didn't make much difference.

I bowed and waited.

"Who are you?" he said.

"A student from Paris, traveling to Oxford in England, asking shelter for the night and a safe-conduct through your territory."

"How did you get here?"

"On foot."

He cursed softly, probably because his men had not been more efficient. "What's your name?" he said and picked up his meat again.

"Heron of Foix."

He puckered his mouth. "From the family of the Count of Foix?"

I wasn't at all of that family but it seemed sensible not to say so.

"I wouldn't dream of taking less than fifty francs from a gentleman like you," the captain stated.

"All I have in the world is twenty francs."

"I'll take those."

"I have a long way ahead of me."

"That's what you think," the captain said, laughing very hard.

I began to laugh too, heaven knows why. That pleased him. "Sit down," he said, "and eat something. I'll take five. You're lucky."

That night, he let me sleep on a bench in his room where there was a big fire. We were awakened at dawn by some of his men bringing in the old winegrower.

"Captain, we found one," they cried. "But he says he has nothing."

"Then cut his throat," the captain grumbled.

"No, don't do that," I said. "I know this man. He has nothing."

The captain sat on the edge of his bed, unbuttoned

his shirt, and started scratching his chest. "They all say that, Foix. They've all got a pot of gold somewhere."

"Not me," the old man cried.

"Then cut his throat," the captain repeated.

"Captain," I said, "this man is the only human being I've found between here and Paris. You can't kill him. Don't you see? He's a link; if you kill him, you no longer control a province of France, you just run around in empty space. You must spare him for your own sake."

The men began to laugh at that word "province." Their captain was obviously only a little captain. The old man gaped at me. The captain lay down and went back to sleep without saying another word.

I left shortly after, my pockets full of bread I'd stolen from his kitchen. He had never asked for the five francs but I had no safe-conduct from him. I didn't think he controlled much area anyway.

I went due north from the house. For a long time I heard behind me the high screams of the old man. They were torturing him in the courtyard, using meat hooks and ropes; I hoped he had a secret to give away.

4
. . . .

IN THE COURSE OF THAT MORNING I ENTERED THE WOODS. IT
wasn't a gradual change: at the edge of a glary field the
trees suddenly began, shadow, and thick undergrowth.
Soon I came upon a path which seemed to go more or less
in my direction, north; it was neglected but not difficult.
I left behind me the wide moat of desolation surrounding the city.

I had come to Paris as a small boy with my mother,
from Hainaut in the north, after my father had died in
the great plague. That was ten years ago. I had lived in
Paris ever since, and everything and everyone I knew
were bound up with that city where my first friends
were, my first books, the first girl who let me make love
to her.

But I felt no regret now, just the opposite: leaving it
all behind was like a liberation.

We in the city knew that the world was dying around
us. Armies and gangs of bandits roamed and fought each
other and everyone else. The king was a prisoner in

England but no one bothered about him except his own clique who tried to raise his ransom from the peasants. The peasants paid and paid and yet they went on growing food. Nothing since the beginning of the world has ever stopped them from doing that. At least not until this very year; this year, unbelievably almost, it truly seemed as if they wouldn't any more.

There had been fighting and burning and plundering before, but what was happening in France now was different: there was no mercy, no ending to it, no idea behind it. Men were like birds with iron beaks, hammering and hammering away at the almost hopeless land. More than half the students were in theology colleges, but there was no Christianity left either. The few who really believed didn't sit in schoolrooms but went into monasteries and vanished from our sight.

Yet it wasn't at all a mood of misery which hung in the streets of the Latin Quarter. The older people, the priests and the professors, ignored what was happening, I think, except where it touched their private interests; when they talked about the outer world, which was rare enough, it sounded as if they were discussing the war between Caesar and Pompey.

And the students just didn't care. We did a lot of drinking and fighting, we argued and read too because through scholasticism we felt superior to the dirt and hunger around us, and we tried to make love to every girl. I don't know what the other students did about confession; I and my friends always went to the same old priest, Father Morel, a great scholar and also as deaf as a post. He peeked hard at you when you stopped talking and if you then smiled in the proper open way he immediately gave absolution.

But I remember a morning at the end of the winter, shortly before I was expelled. We were all sitting in the room of a friend of mine because he had a splendid fire going; some of us were playing cards, others were talking.

There was a lot of shouting and laughter. Wolves came to the Paris cemeteries every night and dug up corpses; now it was suggested that we should stage a wolf hunt. It was the time of the full moon. We'd set out just before nightfall; each of us was to bring a dog, and a sword or a lance or even just a stick. There'd be wine too, to keep warm; and whoever came would later be entitled to wear a hat made of wolf fur. We all became very excited about the plan.

Just then someone who sat near the window shifted his seat and said: "Boys, the snow has turned into rain."

He didn't speak loudly; no one paid attention to his remark. I don't know why his words sounded like thunder to me. They went through me in a shiver; I thought, I have heard them before, I have lived through this before. And: this is what people mean when they say they've heard the voice of God.

I stood up. "I have to leave," I said.

They looked at me; "But you're coming tonight?" someone asked.

I shook my head and left the house.

I came outside and walked to the middle of the street, slipping over the gleaming cobblestones. I looked up at the whiteish sky; the rain was coming down hard now and hit my face. I won't die with the world, I thought; as a matter of fact, neither the world nor I will die; there is something else to be found but not at this dead university and not by hunting wolves in a cemetery. I'll have my hour yet, I'm not going to have it stolen from me; I'll go find it, in spring. I will escape.

I don't know really what came over me that morning; but as I went home in the streaming rain I felt reborn. That was the first time in my life I was consciously happy to be young. I made a song for myself from those words "the snow has turned into rain" and sang it as hard as I could, over the swishing of the rain and the gurgling sound of the bells of the Sorbonne which were ringing in the wet air. The people taking shelter under the gutters of the houses stood staring at me. The water dripped from my hair into my mouth.

And now it was spring, my hour had come, and I was going north through the woods away from Paris and toward the sea.

5

. . . .

I CAME OUT ONTO A GLADE AND HERE A WOMAN WAS CHAR-
ring young green wood. I asked her about the way and
as she said she'd be going presently to take charcoal to a
house up north, I waited and went with her. A big house,
she told me, at two hours' distance. It was called Dammartin and the building intendant of Valois lived there;
he was a strange man.

She was very articulate, but when I asked her had she
always been a charcoal burner, she answered only: "No."

She said that beyond Dammartin the wood ended and
the plain began once more, yet between Dammartin and
a castle on the hill of Montmélian were no houses. I had
told her I was on my way north without adding anything
about England, for that might have sounded odd to her
and made her suspicious about my company. She was
enormous; I had a hard time keeping up with her although she was carrying her load. She didn't even get out
of breath: she walked to the tune of some chant she sang
hoarsely but quite well.

It was already getting dark on the path, and I was stumbling over roots and stones, when we came to the gate of the house. It was smaller than I had imagined from her words, a low stone structure with outbuildings, barely fortified, with a beautiful lawn all around it.

There was no one in sight and no sound but the barking dogs.

I looked at her with some surprise; she shrugged with the same indifference as when I had asked her earlier if she wasn't afraid of wolves. "He lives as if it was peacetime," she said. "I leave you here, sir, goodbye." She opened the gate and vanished behind the house with her charcoal, shouting at the dogs, which fell silent.

I crossed the lawn and looked around me in the dusk. Then I knocked on the front door.

From behind it an old voice called, "Who is it?"

I said I was a student asking lodging for the night. First a peephole, then the door itself opened. It was so dark in the house that I could barely make out the man holding the door.

I thought he'd question me but he said only, "This way if you please."

I followed him blindly through a long corridor and down some steps, and through a courtyard where the evening light still hung, caught between the white walls, into an almost bare room.

"The master of the house is indisposed," he said, "and will not be able to entertain you." He made a slight bow and left; I almost called after him. Suddenly, I felt unbearably lonely.

There was a bunk against the far wall; I sat there until it had become so dark that the grey square of the window no longer stood out. Then I lay down in the blackness and pulled the cover over me. I was cold through and through, and it took me a long time before I stopped shivering.

When I woke, the room was filled with sunlight, and the old man came and led me back down that corridor to what seemed part of a large hall screened off. The furniture consisted of wooden tables and benches. There was a wide window of little glass panels in lead; a man was sitting near it, beside a long table, bent over and looking out on the lawn. When he heard my step he lifted his head and turned a pale sharp face toward me. He made a gesture for me to sit down; there was nowhere to sit very near him and I took a bench at the lower end of his table.

Bread and wine, cheese and meat were brought; before he started eating he said, "I'm the owner of Dammartin House; please feel at home."

"I'm Heron of Foix," I answered, but he did not speak again during his meal.

He ate little and left the room shortly afterward, indicating with a little nod that I should take my time.

I had been afraid to seem greedy and was delighted to be left alone with all that food, for I was starved. I didn't remember ever having sat at such a well-laid table. I seated myself more comfortably, cut a huge slice of the cheese and now started my breakfast in earnest.

The room had been warmed by the sun, the grass outside shone with smoothness, and I was as snug as a prince. When I had finished I didn't stir; I couldn't quite get going again. I poured some more wine; it gave off slow oily reflections in the sunlight.

The house was silent, it was as if my presence had been forgotten.

I fell into a reverie. Traveling to England, I would have to cross the sea, which I had never seen; it seemed to me now as if that sea itself was my destination. I visualized it, a smooth glittering plain of water, slowly canting up and down, boats gliding to and fro, and everyone in them seasick. Everyone but me; I climbed a mast, there was a hard wind in my face, great brightness all around me.

"Good morning," someone said. I looked up into the face of a girl.

6

....

I CANNOT NOW REMEMBER HOW IT FELT TO SEE HER WITH-out knowing who she was. I know I was struck by her eyes, grey-brown, and the copper color of her hair (it was the sunny room which made it that way, her hair is simply dark blond); I remember that for some reason a line from a stupid song sprang to my head, which goes, "and her round high breasts . . ." although she wore a wide and chaste dress; above all she seemed to possess a quality which I'd describe as an overflowing, youthful, luminousness. Perhaps a less biased observer would simply call her a fair-skinned almost plump girl—she isn't plump though—but I know that I decided in that same moment to fall in love with her.

"Good morning," I said, and stood up. Instead of look-ing at her I looked down upon myself and was aware of appearing shabby and ill-kempt. I thought hastily, I must try and get in a romantic explanation of my disheveled state. Just then a maid entered who said to me in an unpleasant tone, "We thought you'd gone, sir. This is the lady of the house, who has to be here."

I didn't think of anything to answer. I bowed and left, walked to the back of the house and came to the kitchens where a cook explained to me the way to Montmélian. I set out hesitantly: I had wanted to talk to the girl.

I got as far as the edge of the lawn. They hadn't built a fence there, the ground dropped away steeply toward the village which was just a collection of miserable huts. Down the slope zigzagged a path, or rather a trail, made through the rushes by the feet of villagers coming and going. I sat down on a rock, but after a while I got up and with a sigh began the descent. Halfway down, my knees buckled and I stopped to rest; when I looked back up I saw the head of the girl against the blue sky. She was sitting where I had sat before. I turned and climbed back.

I worried that she'd be annoyed at that, but when I appeared over the edge she was laughing.

"I hope I'm not being rude," I said.

"To the contrary," she answered, "I wanted you to climb back up. I was bored."

"Why did you laugh?"

"You don't make a very elegant climber."

"That's only because my feet hurt," I said, offended. "I've been on the road for too long."

"Then sit down and talk to me awhile."

"Won't that annoy your father?"

23

"Oh, I shouldn't think so."

I told her about myself. She said little but she listened with a contented air as if to a professional storyteller.

When I announced that I was on my way to Oxford, she asked why.

"It's only a first goal," I answered. "I carry a letter for the dean of Merton College. Did you know that Oxford was founded by exiles from Paris? That was hundreds of years ago. I like the idea of following in their trail. I'm not going to stay there though. I'm going on to—to everywhere."

"You must be a rich man."

I couldn't tell whether she was being ironic. "I've twenty francs on me, and they say it takes ten just to be sailed across the Channel. But that doesn't matter. I made a discovery some time ago. It's hard to talk about it."

"Try," she said.

"I discovered that more than anything else in this world I wanted to be free. And then I found I could be. It's just a matter of daring to. Once I dared, my college, in Paris, no longer seemed a shelter but a prison. Soon after that I wrote a poem for which they threw me out; I had a bad name already for speaking out of turn and thinking wrong thoughts. It suited me perfectly, for I was going to leave in the spring anyway."

"Free," she said.

"Do you like that idea?"

"It frightens me. Free for what, student?" She jumped

up. "I have to go in," she said. "But I enjoyed your story very much."

I stood up too. "What is your name?" I asked.

"Claudia."

I couldn't help smiling at her. "What a lovely, poetic, heathenish name."

She raised her eyebrows. "Poetic?"

"How did your father get the Bishop's consent? It sounds very un-Christian."

"But not at all. I was born on the fifteenth of January. That's Saint Maur's Day. He's the saint of the lame, and 'Claudus' is Latin for 'lame.' "

"Of course," I said. "Forgive me. You're a very learned girl."

She took a few steps toward the house, stood still and looked at me. "Why did you say it was poetic?"

"How old were you on January fifteen last?"

She frowned with irritation, but then she answered, "Sixteen."

"Claudia is a poetic name," I now said, "but I wasn't thinking of a gouty saint; Claudia was the name of a lady of breathtaking beauty who lived in Rome, before Christ was born."

She blushed.

"Her full name was Claudia Pulcher, and every man in the city was in love with her. 'Amata nobis quantum amabitur nulla.' A poet wrote that to her. He loved her most of all."

"What does it mean?"

"Loved by us both as no woman will ever be loved."

She didn't answer any more and walked away.

"But you could be loved that way too," I said softly.

7

. . . .

NO FOOD WAS TO BE FOUND IN THE VILLAGE AT THE BOTTOM
of the slope but it showed a surprising measure of normal
life. There were women and children outside the huts, I
saw hens scratching away in the ditch, and even a cow.
Dammartin was legally part of the household of the King
of France and that's why soldiers and such tended to
avoid it. At least that's what I understood from the con-
fused story a wheezing old villager told me. I had asked
him where I could buy bread and he said, nowhere; after
that I had difficulty shaking him off for he had seen me
descend from the house. He talked and talked at me and
ended up warning me very angrily, though I wasn't quite
sure against what or whom. Finally I got rid of him and
set off to Montmélian.

Far to my right lay the forest of Chantilly, but the
ground there was too hilly and the undergrowth too
thick for traveling. I had to stay in the plain though it
was dangerous; at two places on the horizon I could see
thin columns of smoke rise.

Who could say what was burning there and whether human beings were perishing in those flames? I kept the sun over my left shoulder, going northwest and as close as I could to the wooded area.

I was lucky that day for I saw more fires and they were never near me, and no one stopped me on my way. I didn't think too much about bandits nor even about my feet; I tried to keep all thought but of Claudia out of my mind.

So I came, unexpectedly fast, to a point where the somber tower of the castle of Montmélian loomed behind a strip of almost leafless old elms covering a hillside. I reached the gatehouse shortly after.

It was different here from Dammartin. There were two walls; a sergeant at the inner wall told me that only gentlemen travelers were received at Montmélian. He wasn't even rude, he just wasn't interested. "Call the—" I began but he had already closed the panel in the heavy door.

I walked away. A soldier at the outer gate whistled at me to make me stop. "Don't go down to the village, fellow," he said. "They don't shelter strangers there. Or when they do, they make such a good job of it that you're sheltered till Judgment Day." He moved his thumb across his throat and whistled through his teeth.

So I followed the inside of the wall, and found a recess with no wind and the stone still warm from the sun. I covered myself with my jacket. If I don't think about the cold of the night, I won't feel it, I said.

I realized then that I had nothing which had belonged to Claudia or could be associated with her, and was furious at myself for not having asked or just stolen something which could be a keepsake. I decided I had to find reasons why my meeting her was not mere chance. I wouldn't have seen her if I hadn't stayed so long in that room, I thought, and I stayed only because I had started dreaming about the sea. But the sea is the all-embracing, and the border of the known. Thus it twice symbolizes womanhood. The woman who led me to Dammartin House burned green wood and changed it into charcoal with its lasting glow; that symbolized making love to a maiden. And what had set me on my journey were those words about the snow changing to rain. I had some trouble with that; then I thought that ice changed to water meant a young girl's cold heart melting into a woman's tears through her first love. At this point I discovered that all of this was not stopping me from being wickedly cold and uncomfortable; there was a nauseating smell, too, for all along the foot of the wall litter and garbage had been dumped.

I never saw the village. I began my descent to it at dawn; halfway down the hill a group of riders galloped by me, ladies and gentlemen looking quite splendid. I stood still and stared after them, moved by an odd mixture of envy and nostalgia; I was almost run down by a horseman trailing behind and trying to catch up with the others. I thought, perhaps I'd want wealth too, and a house, and a name in that world, while it lasts.

After that I had to cross the road to Senlis, and here I met a wagon going north. A man rode beside it who looked quite pleasant; he cried cheerfully, "Want to be in Senlis by nightfall, young man?" I had planned to take the Chantilly road but I suddenly couldn't bear the thought of walking another step; I climbed on the wagon, and soon fell asleep.

At sundown we rattled and squeaked through the south gate into the narrow main street of the town of Senlis. We were just in time. The setting of the sun meant curfew; they closed the gate after us and presently the streets lay deserted.

8

....

ON THE MARKET SQUARE OF THAT TOWN STOOD A KIND OF
inn; here I took a room all to myself and ordered a hot
bath prepared without asking prices. I sat in the steaming
water and thought, Heron, you've gone out of your
mind; but I enjoyed it. And then I hit upon the idea of
writing a letter to Claudia. First they told me the roads
were too dangerous for the delivering of letters; but the
following morning an ex-soldier in a quilted coat green
and molded with age, on an even older horse, came
around and said he'd deliver my letter for ten sous.

"And you'll have to pay the same for the answer," he
said.

The answer! I'd never thought of expecting an answer.
But of course there might be one, and I'd wait for it right
there.

To Claudia de Saint-Jean
Dammartin House

I am in love with you.

Not a love to ensnare you but a love to set you free.

I know the world is sick, Claudia. But let it be sick without you or me for a while.

Rise up, my love, my fair one, for the winter is past. That's from the Song of Solomon. And don't let your priest tell you that that song is an ode to the Church. It's an ode to Pharaoh's daughter. She was beautiful, but not as beautiful as you are.

I want to carry your portrait in my heart, on my journey. Let me know that I may. That way I can come back to you safely and serve you.

I will look at no other woman. There is none like you.

Did I feel all this or was it acted, like a story in a romance? A bit of both perhaps; but once I had written those words, seen them in front of me, they assumed a life of their own and became true outside my will.

And it seemed to me when I sealed that letter that I loved Claudia, loved her better than any girl ever before in my life, and that I had loved her that much from the first moment.

9
· · · · · · ·

A WEEK LATER ON A RAINY MORNING I WAS DRYING MYSELF
out in an inn at Abbéville, sitting in my stockings and
drinking beer when that same soldier in the greenish
quilted coat came shuffling in.

He was very sharp: he took a seat right near the door,
with his back toward the wall, and he looked around
carefully before he sat down, but he didn't recognize me.

I had waited two days for him in Senlis before giving
up. I had walked north for five days through Ile de
France and followed the Somme River into Picardy; the
weather had broken and rain kept coming down in hard
spring showers; three nights I had slept in the open in
abandoned ruins. No wonder the soldier didn't recognize
me from the bathed and brushed gentleman who had
given him a letter to take to Dammartin.

He was actually a nasty-looking fellow with a foxy
yellow face, but I didn't think he had played me a trick.
"My courier!" I shouted, extremely pleased, and jumped
up with a smile at him. He stared at me, then walked out

33

of the inn. There was no time to put my boots back on; I ran after him in my stockings. When I came outside he was just mounting his horse. I slithered in the mud. I was bewildered; for a wild moment I imagined that he must have murdered Claudia to run away like that. I picked up a stone and threw it as hard as I could.

My throw met with unexpected success: I hit him square on the back of his head and he fell off his horse. I was on him before he stirred and got hold of his right arm; the left one was pinned behind his back. When he opened his eyes I had my knife out.

He looked at me without uttering a sound; then he made a gesture with his chin toward his breast. I put my knee on his arm and opened his moldy coat. Wound several times around his middle was a blue silk scarf. The scarf was so shiny, the man's blouse so filthy, that just by looking at the two any judge would have hanged him for a thief. "Did the lady give you that for me?" I asked, and he nodded.

He carried a long knife in a sheath at his belt. I grabbed hold of it and jumped away from him, facing him with the two knives. Short of killing him on the spot with my own knife I didn't quite see what else I could have done; luckily for me he wasn't too much of a soldier. He stood up, unwound the scarf, tossed it to me without any expression on his face, and walked toward his horse which was grazing near the ditch.

I went back inside with the scarf. I was covered with

mud but highly pleased with myself. I put it around my neck; one end almost touched the ground. Knights travel like that, wearing the scarves of their ladies; and blue is the color of fidelity.

Claudia was my lady now, and my journey would be in her honor. She couldn't have a lover on foot, I decided. I had to buy a horse, even if I starved for it.

10
. . . .

THE FLAT COUNTRYSIDE OF PICARDY WAS LYING UNDER THE rain, left to itself by men who no longer had the strength to organize it. The water had risen from the choking ditches and spread over the fields. There seemed to be no life present but in weeds, rats, mangy dogs, and wolves; yes, even wolves, not seen for a century in the land of the Northwest. Preying plants and beasts, and birds: clouds of crows kept sweeping and circling over the trees and the lanes, cawing for corpses to alight on, rising and falling in a great rush of wings.

Men-at-arms had parceled up the land, gangster knights like Albrest the Ox and Pierre of Audley, killing the poor farmers and ransoming the rich again and again until they were poor. Half the villages I passed were in ruins; the others had become fortresses. Churches were strongholds, peaked-looking children stood on guard like soldiers. Church bells were rung only to give alarm, whenever a band of armd men came in sight.

Then the peasants fled or barricaded themselves and waited.

I'd hear those bells from far off and it was as if they were rung prophetically for a fire which hadn't yet started: for often some time after the bells a column of smoke, smoke from burning huts, rose in the distance. What peasant would fight back against armed and mounted men, men who fought as a profession?

The peasants withdrew and withdrew, they dug in, they hid, they buried themselves, they made themselves well-nigh invisible; and still the men on horseback returned.

Rain fell, and then the sky cleared again, the sun stood on beams of light in the heavy clouds and a moist stench rose from the land.

It was as if the world, as if the earth itself, were tensely waiting, tired and with bated breath, smarting for deliverance.

II
. . . .

IN ONE DAY I BECAME THE OWNER OF A HORSE AND SAW THE
sea.

The horse was a rather sorry creature, dazed-looking
and so thin that you could follow each rib from beginning to end. But its stomach wasn't swollen, which, I've
been told, is a very good sign, and its walk was easy. That
was important enough for I hadn't been on a horse since
I was ten. I liked her from the start—it was a mare—and
since the dubious fellow who sold her to me (for eight
francs, with saddle and bridle) claimed she had no
name, I decided to call her Melody. My only problem
with her was that she kept shaking her head and pulling
it down, and soon she thus broke one of the badly worn
reins. That took me by surprise and somehow made me
fall off; but it was the only time and she didn't use the
occasion to run away from me. I was now the visible
owner of property worth having my throat cut for, and
I was thankful for the ex-soldier's long knife. When I
went to sleep I held it in my hand.

It was late afternoon when I came to St. Valéry at the mouth of the Somme River but I rode through the village and on. A path led gradually to the top of a dune; the soil here was sandy, shining through the sparse redtop leaves. The hard wind carried a smell of brine and swept deep patterns in the grass. There was a new, an unheard sound in the air.

I came to the top, I hardly dared look; there it was. The sea—very much not a canting glossy plain of water as I'd imagined it, but a wide huge grey swell, waves coming in endlessly, line after line from far out and breaking in foam, gulls crying painfully and a wind which brought tears to my eyes. Opposite me the sun was just visible through a thin cloud layer. Dark clouds, much lower, raced across the sky.

I stood there and stared, and the thought that there was nothing before me but water until the very end of the earth made me dizzy and almost sick to my stomach.

Then I recovered and breathed deeply; and seeing the sea was a triumph.

I WAS COOKING A FISH ON THE BEACH, WHILE THREE GIRLS watched each movement I made. I'd come upon them working on a net spread out on the wide sand of low tide; they had sold me the fish and lent me their fire to cook it on. I couldn't help staring back at one of them. She was hard, very brown, and pretty, and she looked at me with a wicked sweet smile. The other two whispered and giggled. Then they began to sing softly:

> *To give your love*
> *Love and delight*
> *Hold her nude*
> *In solitude*
> *Wind of spring*
> *Please end the night*
> *And bring the rain*
> *A sweet soft rain*

I had been on my way and alone for two weeks now. I suddenly wanted that girl so terribly much that my fish stuck in my throat.

She tilted her head backwards and then she got up and walked away along the beach. And I was sitting there, poking at my hot fish with dead fingers and cursing to myself. And the other two laughed and started all over on their song. I left my fish and rode after her.

When I caught up with her, she stood still. I felt desperate; Claudia, Claudia, I kept saying to myself. But I thought: why act like a knight-errant? I'm only a penniless student on an old nag which was probably stolen in the first place. No one will ever know, Claudia can still be my lady. Yet I couldn't make myself get off the horse.

The girl looked up at me with a serene face, and then she pulled her shawl off one shoulder and showed me her beautiful sharp breast pointed at me. I bent over and took her hand, put a kiss on it and rode off as hard as I could.

After that I saw few human beings during the four days' riding along the ocean beach from St. Valéry to Calais: some fishermen, some naked children playing in the sand. They all stared hard: on my thin sorrel mare, with a glitteringly blue scarf hanging down over my shoulder, I must have made an odd sight. But no one tried to interfere with me.

I went north, with sand and tall grass on my right and the waves on my left, and I was in another world. The second morning of waking up within sight of the sea I had gained a sense of familiarity with it; the sea makes happy. The pureness of the wind along that beach, the soothing roar and the constancy of the waves, made me feel as if I had succeeded in crawling out of an ant hill, a hill of blind human ants incessantly engaged in dragging their bits of loot and food hither and thither, while robbing, fighting and killing the other ants along their way.

I rode and sometimes I walked; I tried to lead Melody into the sea a bit, just a few feet, but she didn't like that, and I sang for myself. The weather stayed dry but the sky was overcast. At times my cheeks became caked with salt in the sharp air, but I didn't suffer from cold.

I dreamt of that girl's face turned up toward me, a brown face with light eyes under shaggy dirty black hair and unbelievably exciting; and even now in dreams her face still returns to me sometimes, although I will never see her again.

13
· · · · · · ·

CALAIS WAS THE PLACE TO FIND A BOAT FOR ENGLAND; I'D
have to do some clever scouting and bargaining there.
The beach does not lead to the town; a few miles to the
south it becomes stony and then cliffs rise from the sea. I
got off and led Melody inland. Behind me the sea lay
dark and very rough.

I came upon a path and rode again; at the crossroads I
found a camp of three covered wagons, with men and
women sitting around a fire. They weren't tramps, they
were musicians, and they invited me to their fire as these
people always do.

I was handed a bowl of barley soup, weird-tasting but
hot, while they all went on talking very excitedly. I listened hard but couldn't make out what it was about:
they were Languedoc people. Finally I asked and with
an attempt at my kind of French they told me they'd
escaped from a battle the day before—they had driven
right through it—a battle between peasants and knights.

I didn't answer, I thought they were playing some elaborate joke on me as a stranger. A man took something out of a bag and showed it to me with a grave face. It was a silver spur; he had taken it from a body.

"Then the peasants killed a knight?"

"They killed nine of them. They won the battle."

If it was a joke, there was little point to it; I was surprised enough but no one laughed at me. When I left they were still talking away and hardly looked up to see me go.

Calais was quiet and without visible scars of war; its arched cobblestoned streets seemed empty and its houses huddled as if blown together by the high wind. I rode to the quarter of the fishermen, which lay outside the walls; I was glad when I saw the sea reappear ahead of me. I missed you, I told her, I've become a foster child of yours.

There was a sharp smell of fish and salt in the air; the sky was a hurtful glaring grey.

I asked about boats and a large hut was pointed out to me at the edge of a dune where men were working on a net.

"He wants to go to England," one of them said when I appeared.

"That costs ten francs," another answered.

I coughed and said, "I've got five."

The first speaker grunted. "Ten," he said.

"Can't you do it for five?" I asked. "I'm not haggling, I haven't got more."

No one answered; during the conversation no one had looked at me.

Riding down to a kind of sailor's inn I asked the advice of an old man who was taking care of the horses. He told me to hang around awhile.

And so I was sitting in that inn when a horseman in high boots entered, very flushed; he looked like a gentleman but they all knew him. "Listen to this," he cried, "the peasants of Saint-Leu have taken the castle, by storm, like soldiers!"

"The castle of Saint-Leu?" the landlord said. "That's near Paris."

"Yes, near Paris," the horseman affirmed impatiently. "Can you believe it? Taken by the scum of the village, an army with sticks and stones, soldiers in armor of dirt!" He began to laugh uproariously and then he said, looking at each of us in turn, "All the military on the road are talking about it. They say it's an evil portent of some sort."

That afternoon I went all over town but I couldn't find a soul who'd take me across the Channel for less than ten francs. The old hostler from the inn had vanished.

The rumor was spreading now about the peasants in Ile de France who had taken a castle. Everyone told it differently; and if the castle was Saint-Leu, how could my musicians have seen the battle only a day before? Perhaps they had made up their story to cover the theft of that spur.

45

Back in the inn I found the same men still hanging around. They had settled for this version: a nobleman of Saint-Leu had raped a peasant's daughter, a pious maiden preparing to enter a convent. While the villagers were praying for her, Saint Michael had appeared and led them to the house of the knight. The nobleman and his servants came out but when they saw the Archangel their arms were paralyzed, they dropped their swords, and the peasants killed them all. Indeed, a miracle was needed to explain such a happening.

I slept in the inn.

Early in the morning the hostler called me out and showed me to a one-armed sailor. This man was willing to take me across for five francs if I'd help him with his boat. His son was away; he needed someone to load and unload his wares. "I'll carry your horse too," he said, "but you'll have to leave that long knife behind, I don't want that in my boat." So I had found my passage, and quite easily.

Before noon the sky suddenly blew clear. We worked on the beach in the dazzling sunlight and the pleasing smell of sun on the tar and ropes of his little boat. We didn't work hard but before sunset most of the job was done. "I'll sail tomorrow in the afternoon," my captain said.

In the town people were still discussing the peasants' feat of arms but I didn't join in. I was not concerned, I had a boat now, I was to leave this land the very next day.

I was no longer involved in their deadly games. I was bound for the sea.

The night was restless and haunted. I tossed on my bunk at the back of the inn and I heard shouting in the street, clanking of arms, strange clamor. Then there were heavy steps and the clop of horses' hoofs, but the sound passed by and vanished.

As I opened my eyes at dawn I saw the horseman in his high boots straddle the middle of the room. The inn was already crowded, people were sitting everywhere. It must have rained before sunrise; a bitter smell of wet clothes hung in the air. In a raw voice, as if repeating something they had agreed upon, that man said to the company: "The peasants have risen to destroy the world."

14
. . . .

MERCENARIES OF THE ENGLISH ARMY HAD DESCENDED ON
the town in the night, stragglers from pitched battles
in which peasants had massacred professional soldiers.
They came from different provinces and their bloody
stories, pieced together, gave a picture of the whole countryside rising and somehow getting the better of the sol-
diery. I didn't doubt that some peculiar incidents were
thus exaggerated into an Armageddon, for soldiers have
chosen a profession of sin and thus are forever in the
need of justifying themselves with tales of impossible
danger and unlikely courage. Yet I couldn't help feeling
some contempt for the people of Calais, haggard fishers
and sailors whose toiling on the water isn't so different
from the peasants' toiling on the earth: they were shouting in that inn as if they themselves were lords and as if
their own serfs were defying them. I hastened to leave
the place.

Outside it was a clear lovely morning with a sea bluer
than I had ever seen it before. My skipper was sitting on

a log of wood eating his gruel and he greeted me warmly; we had got along well the day before.

Two soldiers had come to offer him money for a passage to England, he told me. He had refused, he would never willingly let an armed man into his boat.

We finished the storing of his wares, and sat around waiting for the tide. He offered me some gruel; then he dozed off.

There must have been twenty or thirty soldiers in the town; they came by on foot in twos and threes. They behaved very calmly; their voices were soft against the hammering of the boat builders and distant swish of the surf. When I close my eyes I can still see that scene in every detail, and it is as if I feel again the grains of sand the wind blew against my face.

My skipper nodded in his sleep, and then the step of a soldier going close by in heavy boots made him sit up straight and open his eyes.

He looked at me. "Are they Englishmen?" I asked him.

The skipper shrugged. "They're from everywhere. One who was here this morning came from Valois."

"Hell and damnation," I said sharply and he gave me a surprised stare.

I had known there was a connection. I had known events were threatening me; but I had resisted that knowledge. Why, why had that damned old man said that, about the soldier being from Valois? Hadn't I asked only whether they were English or not? Why tell me?

I walked down the sunny street and came upon a priest; not a village priest, he was too well turned out for that. I asked him in Latin about Saint-Leu.

He was a thin priest. I think I prefer fat ones. My Latin didn't take him in, he looked at me with arrogant eyes. "God will punish those peasants, my son," he said.

He wanted to walk on and I took hold of his sleeve. "What is happening, Father?"

"The rabble," he said, and his eyes included me in that word, "have risen in Ile de France province. They have burned houses and castles. But several princes have already assembled to cut them down."

"Which houses were burned?"

"Dammartin, Thoix, Catheux."

I knew he'd say Dammartin.

I turned around and walked back to my captain. He saw me coming but I looked past him at the sea which was so very blue that day.

"I can't come with you after all," I said when I stood near him.

He only answered, "I can't pay you for the work you've done."

I loosened Melody's rope, I climbed on heavily and rode down that street. I took the road inland to the southeast. The sun shone in my eyes, the sea was behind me; I didn't look back.

15
. . . .

I HAD NOT KNOWN THAT ONE CAN LOVE AND HATE SOME-
body at the same time. As I rode back toward Dammartin I felt death in my heart and I hated Claudia. Why in
Jesus' sweet name couldn't she leave me alone, I thought.
At the very same time I was aware of the wild unreason-
ableness of that; she hadn't asked me anything, least of
all to love her or to come back for her. More strange still,
I knew quite well that this love for a girl I had hardly
seen, never touched, was largely something I had created
alone, in my own mind.

I think such creation is legitimate; it gives a hold to a
man who sets out on an undertaking all alone in this
chaotic world. But wasn't it foolishness to let it lead to a
fatal decision, to risk having my throat cut for it? Perhaps not, perhaps a man can do nothing more noble than
to give as much reality to an idea as he does to a rock or a
knife wound. In any case, I never considered turning
around again to the sea.

The people had indeed risen—but as far as I perceived not against their masters; they had simply risen as if from the underground. On my fast way back through Artois and Picardy I saw more men, women and children in the fields and on the roads in one hour than before in a day; where had they all come from? I saw them patching up skeletons of huts with branches and reeds, and what was an even more pathetic sight, I saw fields being sown although it would be very much too late in the season for a harvest. They acted as if peace had descended on the land; and everywhere there was the same wild story rampant—that the king had been released by the English and was on his way to form an army of his people which would bring peace to the country.

Farther south the landscape became more grim with peasants building barricades on village roads and even practicing archery. But here too the professional soldiers and the marauders seemed to have vanished from the earth.

Four days brought me to Senlis. In that town the talk was of the valley of the Marne: only there the peasants had taken to arms and burned the houses of the gentry. No one seemed to know whether they had dispersed after that and no one was really certain of anything. But it was here that I was told that Dammartin hadn't been burned at all. Who would dare touch the property of the king's building intendant, they said.

When I heard that, I didn't think: "I've come back for

no reason." A shock of happiness ran through me; I thought, of course I had to see Claudia again, I'm wearing her scarf, she is my lady, that pledge has to be made in person. She must see me on horseback.

My resentment against her melted away now that she turned out not to be in need of my help after all. My going back to see her became a romance. And I began to tell myself secretly, perhaps she'll even come away with me.

It was less than a day's ride to Dammartin now. Then, as during the first part of that journey, I was so obsessed with my goal that I paid little attention to the world around me. I wasn't careful, I didn't plan, I felt well-nigh invulnerable and invisible.

My approach to Dammartin was from the north this time. The road climbed gradually; so suddenly did I come upon the fence of the house that it took me unawares.

The lawn was there, and it was as green and smooth as the first time I had seen it. But where the house had stood was a charred ruin.

16

....

IT WAS AS IF I HALTED THE REALIZATION OF WHAT HAD HAP-
pened somewhere between my eyes and my mind; and
in that twilight state I tethered Melody to the fence. She
was so exhausted that she tried to lie down. I rubbed her
neck for a moment and whispered some words of conso-
lation, oh you poor creature, I said. Then I crossed the
lawn and stood in front of those stones and ashes. I
placed my hand on them and the ashes were cold, as
cold as if this fire had burned long long ago. And then
the bitter taste began to rise in my mouth.

But I couldn't leave Dammartin House. I wandered
and poked around in the ruins; there was nothing to be
found. Later, in the empty street of the village, I felt a
hatred in me as sharp as a thorn, "They must be crushed,
they must be punished," I kept saying aloud, standing in
the mud amidst the abandoned huts.

For four or five days I rode around in the Valois. I was
now told that an army of peasants was on the march, an
army of thousands and thousands—no, a hundred thou-

sand of them—rabble gone mad, destroying everything in their path like the locusts of Egypt. But no one knew where this army was. No one knew about the building intendant of Valois.

An uneasy quiet hung low over the land here.

Late one day as I rode up to an abbey, Melody stumbled. I got off just before she fell. I stroked her forehead, but she didn't stir.

She was dead.

A gatekeeper let me in at the abbey and took me to the hall. There were no monks present; at a table in a corner a group of women and children were seated.

"They're refugees from the peasants," he whispered.

I approached the table. A girl in black, with a black woolen scarf all around her head, turned and looked at us. It was Claudia.

17

·······

DAMMARTIN HOUSE WAS DESTROYED BY A GANG OF PEASANTS
who had strayed from the main body moving up the Oise
River. It was in the valley of the Oise, not of the Marne,
that the rising had started: and it was true that thousands
of men were still marching. It was now even said that
the people of Paris were sending out help to these rebels.

Claudia's father must have known about the rebellion
but he had not said a word to her. In his own village all
was quiet. Thus this unheard-of and final breakdown in
the order of man had come upon her like a cursed dream.
As she was sitting under the trees, not far from the
house, a herd of peasants had suddenly appeared on the
lawn. They surrounded the house. What frightened her
most was their silence; she stood behind a tree, petrified.
Then, in a matter of seconds, it seemed, smoke and flames
began to rise in several places; her father came out of the
front door; the troop opened as if to let him through; he
walked quite possessed to the stables; at the edge of the
crowd several men attacked him from the rear and cut

him down with swords and scythes. Then Claudia just turned and ran. She went back the following day, for when she opened her eyes in the light of morning and found herself lying in the wood, she had thought that all had been a hallucination. But when she came to the house there was nothing and no one left but smoldering wood, and stones, and her dog lying dead under the trees.

And now she was sitting in a corner of the cold abbey hall, whispering feverishly to me, and I was not even sure she knew who I was. But she talked to me, so fast and low that I could only hear half, and she stroked her blue scarf which I was wearing. A message had gone out to a relative in Paris to come for her, but she didn't want that, she wanted to go to a nunnery. "God hates the world," she whispered. "God hates the peasants. I hate them too."

I put her head against my shoulder and just held her, and she began crying and cried and cried.

The hall became dark and empty, but no one bothered us. And as I sat there I could feel no hatred or anger or love but only an unfathomable pity, pity for Claudia and pity for every man and woman in this silly world. "You'll see," I kept saying to her, "all will be well. You'll see. I'll dry your tears."

18

. . . .

THOSE TERRIBLE WORDS "GOD HATES THE PEASANTS" CLAUDIA
had heard from the abbot. He repeated them that night
in a chapel as dank as a vault, with its only light coming
from a candle on the altar. So suddenly did he shift from
the Latin Mass to those words spoken to the women and
children and me standing in the dark on the rough stone
floor that my mind played me a trick and it seemed to me
for a while that the French he was continuing in was a
strangely soft Latin which I did not understand.

"All displeases the peasant," the abbot said, "he does
not share our joy in Creation. He hates good weather and
he hates rain. He hates his duty, and he hates God when
He does not do what the peasants demand of Him. And
so God hates him in turn and would be satisfied to see
him eat thistles and thorns, and starve, and go naked on
all fours. Whatever he has more is mercy, not right.

"Without God's love," he said, "the peasants have
fallen under the sway of the Devil and abandoned their
condition. The world is a cathedral and each stone has its

place. And its only reason for existence is that place, chosen by the divine Builder Christ. And thus a stone which does not stay in its place has lost its reason for existence, and will be pulverized."

He spoke quite calmly and in a detached voice.

"By raising his hand the peasant has sinned against the Church, Christ, and the Holy Spirit. So rest assured, women and children, for you are here as martyrs of the Church and will be revenged."

I remembered the hatred I had felt against the peasants when I was standing in the empty muddy village of Dammartin. But it hadn't been like this, not like this iron hatred of the mind.

I stopped listening to the abbot and my thoughts turned to the incident of the bread. It had happened in Paris. One morning on our way to the university we found a large crowd collected in front of the bakery which supplied the Latin Quarter. It wasn't a shortage of bread which had brought them to the place: there was no resigned waiting but excitement and alarm. "A miracle," we heard it said, and "A terrible omen!"

The bread had come out of the oven that morning the color of ashes. It was being passed around, stared at, touched; but no one dared taste it. A priest was sent for; he looked at it for a long time and left again without speaking.

All during that day the consternation and horror of the people over the ash-colored bread mounted. Later, when a deafening tumult was heard in the street, we went back to the bakery to see. They had brought in the peasant whose wheat had been used for the bread.

When we had come close enough to watch what was going on, we saw that he had been bound and was held to the ground by several men. Another man forced him to eat the bread; first the peasant tried to chew and swallow but soon this became impossible for him. A woman knelt beside his head and pushed in more bread while the man held the peasant's mouth open; "I'm good at feeding children," she cried. A violent spasm went through the peasant's body which almost shook him free from his captors, then he choked and died. Slowly the crowd dispersed.

We had a debate in our lecture room over this bread; had its color been a bad omen or not? The lecturer came in but did not interrupt; after a while he said, "It was no miracle, I have seen this before. There's an herb called roivolle which sometimes grows with the wheat. It does not stand out in the flour; but the baked bread is turned dark grey by it." He was a country man, from Lorraine.

His words ended the debate but they shocked those of us who had seen that peasant choke to death on the bread. A boy was sitting next to me, I don't think he was more than fifteen; he looked at me placidly and shrugged. "It's nobody's fault that that fellow was born a peasant," he said. "And a peasant is just as well off dead as alive."

19

. . . .

THE FIRST TIME I SAW CLAUDIA LAUGH AGAIN WAS AT OUR
departure from the abbey.

We had talked together a great deal during our few
days there, but in a neutral sort of way. A love letter and
a scarf as a pledge had been exchanged between us; and it
is very awkward to come eye to eye with a girl after
things like that if you don't know each other at all well.
But the death of Claudia's father and the loss of her home
loomed so large that everything else was delegated to
Limbo. There was a kind of understatement in our quiet
conversations; we both felt there was something more,
waiting to be freed, and this feeling, I think, gave us some
happiness in those hours.

Then Claudia told the abbot that I was her cousin who
had been searching for her and would now take her to
Paris. I didn't know whether she really expected me to
do that or would go to a convent or perhaps even be willing to accompany me on another sortie to England and
Oxford. I knew that was a wild idea; when I brought it

up, as circumspectly as I could, she hadn't answered. She was more herself now, no longer very sad, but distracted; and never as keenly present as that first day when she listened to me on the lawn of Dammartin in the sun. We said as little as possible about practical matters or money. No new refugees had come to the abbey and no news from the outside world. Our main sensations in that place were cold and hunger, for the monks gave us very little to eat.

The morning came when we took leave. The abbot was one of those men who are unaware of other people's antipathy, or he just didn't care. Anyway, he was painfully polite to me; he conducted us to the door and there discoursed to me at great length about the need for courage and prudence on our way to Paris. Claudia shifted from one foot to the other, then suddenly clutched her stomach with the strangest expression on her face.

I thought she had a cramp but when she saw that I was going to ask something, she shook her head violently to shut me up. Luckily the abbot looked only at me; his back was half turned toward her. At last he ended his sermon, we bowed to him and expressed our gratitude and the gatekeeper led us out. Claudia walked faster and faster down the path; she was shaking and I took her hand to comfort her. Then I saw that she wasn't crying but laughing soundlessly.

The gate closed behind us. She fell in the grass, completely out of breath with laughter. "Claudia, what on earth has come over you?" I asked.

She had a very sweet laugh. She couldn't speak, she only shook her head and tears ran down her face. I sat down beside her; finally she brought out: "Just when he said Providence would come to our aid, my candlesticks came loose . . ."

"Your candlesticks?"

She jumped up and shook her dress, and two huge silver candlesticks fell out of it into the grass.

I looked perplexed and she began to laugh again.

"That wicked old man!" she cried, "all the donations we used to make—all that advice of his—and he never offered us a sou for the journey—he said we should look to the Church for support—and so I did."

I jumped up too and kissed her, I was so pleased with her; she kissed me back.

20
. . . .

THEY HAD TOLD US TO HEAD FOR A HOUSE OF THE DOMINICAN
order as a first stage on our road to Paris. I certainly didn't
want to set foot in Paris; I had the feeling that if I did, I'd
never get out again. But we took our direction to that
house—it was almost due west rather than south, anyway—really to postpone the need for decisions. We were
on undefined terms with each other.

We walked that day over lightly wooded ground. The
eastern Valois is lovely country. It was very quiet, there
was only the sound of our feet shuffling through the dead
leaves; the air had the mildness of early summer. Soon
Claudia got tired, and we did not make much progress.
There was something of a dream about that slow march.

A babel of voices was heard just before we came upon
the house of the Dominicans. We stood still and watched.
It was a large low building almost hidden by a wall of
rough stone blocks; not a monastery proper, for Dominicans come and go as they please. A crowd was milling
around at the gate: refugees, some of whom had got

there on carts or horses, others who were on foot. I wanted to go nearer but Claudia held me back. A group of monks were standing in the gateway, obviously deciding who could come in and who could not. The people pushed; men cursed, women cried, children screamed. It was a depressing spectacle.

"I don't want to go there," Claudia said.

"But you're Claudia de Saint-Jean. They'll bow you in."

"Would you go there if you were alone?"

"No, I wouldn't," I said. "I don't like crowds when there is trouble. I can't bear their undisciplined misery."

"Well, neither can I. I'm not undisciplined."

"But with you it's simply that you can't spend the night in the open air."

"If you can, I can," she said.

So we gave the Dominicans a wide berth and walked on. We were very lucky; before darkness our path led by a little squatty tower of brick, with most of its pointed roof still on. I peeked through the doorway; it was empty. Weeds grew on the earthen floor. I stamped around a bit; there was some rustling and a fat rat scurried out. Claudia screamed and then laughed. I carried leafy branches in and handfuls of pine needles and made a bed which was quite soft.

We lay next to each other and covered ourselves with my jacket and Claudia's cape.

We didn't speak. Through the door opening we could

see the western clouds burning with the sunset; then it quickly grew dark. "Look," Claudia said and pointed at a star which shone through a hole in the roof. She turned her back toward me. "I'm cold," she said.

I moved closer and put one arm around her. She fell asleep; I heard her breath become slow and regular. I lay like that, with my body against hers, warm now, wanting her, but very chaste; I could feel her hard girlish lines through all her clothes.

In the morning she said to me in a resolute voice, "I think I don't want to sit around somewhere and bewail the wickedness of the world. I want to be free too. I'll come with you to England." We were standing in the tall wet grass outside our tower when she spoke those words. I remember I was shivering from the cold of the dawn air; but as soon as she had said that I felt wonderfully warm, and I didn't know what to answer; all I could do was grin at her like a cat.

And so I set out a second time for Calais and the sea.

CLAUDIA WAS THE FIRST GIRL I EVER KNEW, OR ANYWAY THE first pretty girl, who could read and think like a man. Her father had taught her, and she had perused all his manuscripts and was full of theories and ideas. But he had not let her read the Romance of the Rose.

I told her that poem as well as I could: about the knight in the mystical garden looking for the Rose, and helped in his quest by a bevy of girls called Hope, Sweet Thought, Sweet Speech, Humble Request, Lawful Pursuit, and names like that.

"Then three women appeared in the garden and they were called Danger, Fear, and Shame. They tried to chase the knight out, and it seemed they would succeed, when powerful allies came to his aid: Venus, and Nature herself. Nature sent her priest to preach for her; 'I have come to excommunicate all enemies of love,' the priest announced, 'for Nature does not wish a woman to be content without a man, nay, she doesn't wish a woman to be content with one single man. Virgins and prudes will all be sent to hell.'

"When he had spoken those words, Venus threw her taper down from the sky. And the taper set the garden, the castle in the garden, country and towns, the whole universe, on fire; but its flames are invisible.

"And once that fire was lit, one of those girls, this one's name was Welcome, led the knight to the place where the Rose grew, and she allowed him to pluck it."

Claudia didn't say anything and I began hesitantly, "The rose stands for—"

She blushed. "I know," she said, rather annoyed.

Much later she suddenly told me, "But I think that pure love is nobler than mixed love."

"I'm not sure you understand them."

"Of course I do," she said vehemently, "pure love is pure, and mixed love is . . . is love consummated. Pure love is spiritual, and mixed love is animalistic. You and your roses—a rose should be looked at, it shouldn't be plucked. When it's plucked, it dies."

"That's just an image," I began hastily, "desire doesn't die when—"

"Desire is beautiful only when you don't stoop to it."

I made a face.

"Perhaps a student can't understand those things," she said.

"You think one has to be an aristocrat to feel that way."

"Yes."

I didn't answer and I accelerated my step; soon she fell behind. I told myself the only humiliation in this would be if I myself felt humiliated.

I came to a crossroads and sat down on a rock; Claudia took quite a while in catching up.

I wanted to continue but she knelt near me and put her hands on my knees like a suppliant. "Please forgive me," she said.

I smiled at her.

"You wrote to me, 'I'm in love with you,' she said. "Was it true?"

I nodded.

"Are you still?"

I took her by her elbows and made her stand up. Claudia had looked pale and haggard when I found her; since we'd left the abbey the color had returned to her face. I studied her; she suppressed a smile and for a moment her teeth gleamed in her mouth, excitingly but also as innocently as they do with children.

"My letter was to an idea girl," I said, "an idea girl and an ideal girl. But I think you and she are the same person."

"Well, I sent my blue scarf to a real person in the first place," she said, "and you are him."

"Why did you?"

"Why?—I don't know—perhaps because you're so tall—and then on our lawn you were so serious, but in a gay way—I only knew boys who are silly in a serious way."

I bowed.

"That's why I got angry at your poem," Claudia said, "you made me feel like a foolish child. I can't help it that I'm a virgin; if that condemns me to hell, so be it."

Now she looked as if she were going to cry a bit but she decided against it.

I took her hand and we went on. We must have made a strange spectacle to any soldier or peasant who saw us go by, strolling through Valois as if it were a pleasure park.

But we didn't see anyone and we didn't look.

It seemed to me then as if Claudia's eyes shone as they had in Dammartin. What had come over us there was the shock of meeting, for me the shock of seeing a lovely girl's face for the first time, or for her a man whose appearance pleased her—so she had just said; now it was all different. Now there was a feeling with a reality of its own, above words and ideas, the feeling of being together, here and in actuality, and without a known time limit to it. I thought: that feeling is an ingredient of real love, and I thought that real love was made up of those two things, opposites: shock and permanence.

That evening a woodman gave us his hut to sleep in and a meal, all for one sou. There were two bunks. Before we went to sleep she let me put my arms around her and kiss her.

THE PHILOSOPHERS, LOOKING NO DOUBT IN SOME ALEXAN-drian manuscripts rather than at the women around them, divided love into amor purus and amor mixtus; Claudia and I now traveled under the flag of amor purus. Her reading had told her that "pure love" was an exalted sentiment which freed the soul from bodily ballast. She was too intellectual a girl to tinker with an established concept, and the concept allowed all but the "physical possession of the beloved." Actually her shyness stopped her well before that—which she explained by saying that it takes time for the body to obey the mind. To me it all seemed more like highly refined torture and also the surest way to become intensely preoccupied with that bodily ballast. But since her outburst over the "Romance of the Rose" I didn't question her ideas any more. I obeyed like a good knight in a story. Claudia was very certain of how things should be, certain in the fascinating and innocent way of children teaching the rules of some complicated game to a newcomer without ever permitting any doubt about the logic and the need of each of those rules.

For a girl who had spent her life within the sheltering walls of a royal mansion, she was very tough. We didn't eat hot food or sleep in a house until we came to Crépy-en-Valois, an old and decrepit little town which ignored what was going on around it to an impressive degree. In Crépy, Claudia marched without hesitation into the shop of the goldsmith and put her two stolen candlesticks on his table. The goldsmith eyed us with suspicion, as well he might for we were beginning to look like tramps. Finally he said, "I don't want to buy your stuff. And the two of you better get out of our town before we lock you up."

Claudia didn't grow angry; her face showed that she couldn't be angered by a tradesman. "Good fellow," she said in the thinnest most supercilious voice any lady ever employed, "these candlesticks were saved for me when a mob pilfered our possessions. I will not sell them, for no one in my family sells; I will leave them here in pledge against such a sum as you tell me is proper."

The goldsmith took off his little cap and inspected the sticks much longer than necessary; he had completely lost his aplomb. We left with a ten-franc gold piece, which Claudia with a gesture indicated I should carry. She had become so much the noble lady in that shop that she frightened me too.

We had a room alone in the inn of Crépy, the only

room there was besides the tap room where some traveling merchants were drinking and snoring. It had a
window of oilcloth, and a rush candle which had been
tied to a stone jutting out from the wall. Even in the half
dark it was obvious how filthy everything was.

Claudia remained standing in the middle of the floor,
looking very ill at ease. "I'd rather sleep in the woods,"
she murmured. Then she began to cry. "I don't know
what I'm doing here," she sobbed. "I should have gone
to Paris."

"It's not too late now," I said lamely. "I'll take you to
your family."

She stopped after a while and smiled at me through
her tears. "I have no family left," she said. "There's no
one, no one except you who are my lover."

"Can you make that candle burn brighter?" she asked
and began taking off her clothes.

I stared, and she sniffed away her last tears and
laughed.

"Since you're my lover," she then stated very seriously, "I'll let you see me this evening. But you're not to
touch me, you know that."

And so Claudia put the bed cover on the dirty floor
near the window and stood on it naked. First she did not
know what to do with her hands but then she folded
them behind her head and posed quite beautifully. There
had been girls in Paris brazen enough to let you make
love to them in the light of day, but I had never looked

73

at a nude girl in such strange circumstances. It was like looking at a statue; Claudia was built like a nymph, with long thighs, a flat belly, high breasts closer together and rounder than one sees in paintings but more lovely because of that, and a smooth skin. It was a breathtaking thought that this entity of beauty, hidden in rather weathered linens, was traveling with me. She was so clear and ingenuous that for that brief time I was won over by the ideal of pure love and worshiped her as a perfect creation instead of desiring her.

Lying next to her in the ramshackle bed in the dark, with most of our clothes on, was more difficult; I was haunted by her image now and cursed all philosophers and the girls who live by them. But she had acquired a new power over me and I no longer felt just the older and the wiser one; I was aware of an intense need to please her and gain her respect.

23
. . . .

IN THAT INN AN ELEGANT YOUNG MAN—OR, BETTER PER-
haps, boy—in a very fine coat came to pay his respects to
Claudia. He had recognized her before she had noticed
him. He was Robert of Lorris, son of Robert of Lorris,
Lord of Ermenonville. When Claudia introduced me as
a cousin escorting her, he smiled, but very open and
pleasantly, as if he would be delighted over our happiness
if we were more than just cousins. I liked him for that.
He couldn't have been much older than Claudia, but
he had so much bearing and manner that I felt a sting of
envy.

Was his home safe, Claudia asked, and he reddened
fleetingly when he said yes, it was.

At that point I told myself I should stop being so care-
less and make more careful provision for our route
ahead: it wouldn't do to stretch the luck Claudia and I
had had so far. So I asked him about the area. The peasants had armed themselves, he said, there were no pro-

fessional troops around and there was little fighting. He seemed rather indifferent about it all.

"How do you know that Ermenonville is safe?" Claudia asked again.

He shrugged. "I just know. And I'd be honored to offer its shelter to Claudia de Saint-Jean, and to you, sir."

Claudia looked at me. She made a face like a naughty schoolgirl, I thought she'd stick her tongue out. "We're going to England," she said, succeeding in surprising Robert of Lorris.

"But it's impossible now to cross the Oise Valley," he said, "it's much too dangerous for you."

"Why?"

"They're fighting in that valley. And the peasants have taken or burned most of the castles. They're raping every woman they get hold of."

Claudia's face darkened. For a moment the expression came back in her eyes I had seen there when I found her in the abbey. "Why does no one beat them down?" she asked.

Lorris didn't answer.

We decided to go with him to Ermenonville for the time being. He was on foot too.

It was as if a spell was broken, with Claudia and me no longer alone; I became aware of the landscape and saw it changing. Perhaps Crépy just happened to be at the edge of the fighting: but that day I saw columns of smoke again, burned-out huts, dogs and crows fighting over rotting corpses of horses. Once Robert and I by common accord took Claudia's arms and directed her attention away from a tree in which a hanged man was dangling, naked and with his eyes pecked out.

Ermenonville and Dammartin had been close neighbors; and she and Robert talked about all sorts of things I knew nothing of. I suddenly appeared to myself as slightly ridiculous and superfluous.

We spent the night in the house of a priest; in the dark I tiptoed over to Claudia to kiss her good night but she whispered for me to go away; she didn't want Robert of Lorris to see.

I lay awake most of that night, between snatches of dreams in which I saw Robert and Claudia embrace and make love and from which I woke in a panic, not knowing what was dreamt and what was true, trying to hold my breath and listen to any sound in that room but only hearing the pounding of the blood in my ears.

I was intensely grateful for the first grey light of dawn and went outside. The grass was too wet to sit in but I found a seat in a gnarled tree. There I sat, shivering, with my arms around my knees, and thinking of the blue sea of Calais I had turned my back on. It was a long time before Claudia and Robert of Lorris came outside, together, and laughing. For a moment I thought of staying out of sight until they were gone, and I was almost disappointed when Claudia halted and called my name.

We had walked for about an hour when Robert

stopped at a little bridge across a stream. "I know a short cut here," he said. "We're getting near Ermenonville."

"Robert," Claudia asked, "I want to know *why* Ermenonville is safe from the peasants."

"Claudia—" I began, but neither of them paid attention to me.

"Dear Claude," Robert said, "you don't know how sad I was when I heard about your father, and Dammartin. But you must understand that in times—"

"Why, Robert?" she asked again.

"Because my father has joined the peasants' cause," Robert said.

We both stared at him.

Robert was unperturbed. "He resigned his rank and is leading one of their armies."

Claudia had become so pale that her face looked leaden and almost ugly. Now for the first time she turned to me and said hoarsely, "Do something, you fool. Heron!"

I didn't answer.

"Do something!" Claudia cried at me, "challenge him, kill him! A man who has betrayed his class! Have you no honor? You—you student!"

I shrugged. "First of all, he's not his father," I began, "and then I'm not so certain that the peasants don't have . . ."

I could not finish my sentence: Claudia slapped my face, and then she walked away in the direction we had come. Robert of Lorris did not wait to see what I would do; he crossed the bridge and left me standing there alone.

After a while I followed Claudia. I caught up with her soon enough; we continued together on our way, but in unbroken silence.

24

AT A FORK IN THE ROAD I STOPPED AND TOLD HER I WAS TAK-ing the northern branch through the King's Wood, the most direct road to Calais—peasants or no peasants. "May I still come with you?" Claudia asked. I nodded and marched on. Claudia stayed beside me, half running every now and again, and she kept looking at me. She was all of a sudden acting like a pet dog.

"I'm only blaming myself," I finally said. "Any man is a fool who chooses for his lady a girl who should still be playing with dolls."

Claudia didn't answer.

"You'd be surprised how much even a student under-stands about women," I said to her. "After one day Robert of Lorris had already taken my place with you. That's what caused that wild outburst of yours at the stream this morning."

"It's not so," Claudia began, but I felt bitter, mainly at myself for not being too proud to talk about this, and I walked on even faster without looking back at her.

That afternoon's march was the most wearisome of my whole journey. Under a dark sky it was warm and humid, and low shreds of cloud seemed to hang in the very tops of the trees. My boots hurt me so that I tried going barefoot; where the ground was covered with pine needles it was cool and soothing but on other places broken branches and pebbles made every step a torture. I came to a pool and here I bathed my feet and put my boots back on. When twilight fell we were still under the trees; swarms of gnats came out and flew into our eyes and mouths. I'm sure one word of sympathy from me would have made Claudia break into tears, but I didn't even look at her. There was only a shimmer of moonlight falling through the ragged clouds and it was already dark when we came upon an empty hut. I cut my bread in two, handed Claudia her piece, and lay down in the far corner, my knife in my left hand, my bread in the other.

I woke with a start in the night. Claudia was lying beside me and pressing her mouth against mine. It was so dark that I couldn't distinguish her face, but I felt that she was shivering. I put my arm around her, and drew it back with a shock, for she was nude.

"Claudia," I whispered and held her against me, because she was trembling so.

She began plucking at my clothes; I felt for her hands to stop her but she pushed my arm away, "I want you to," she said quite loudly. "But I don't want it like this," I whispered, "you're not yourself, what about your theory of pure love ?" She did not heed me, she went on undressing me and finally I couldn't stop myself from helping her with that. And I lay on her, in a bottomless dark, and she pushed her hand between us and brought me into her body. She made a little sound and then I had her; stars and flashes of white light danced before my tightly closed eyes as Claudia de Saint-Jean let herself be taken by me.

25

. . . .

IN THE MIDDLE OF THE DAY WE FOUND OURSELVES BACK AT
Crépy. I don't know how it had happened; I must have
taken a wrong turning. Another surprise was in store for
us: the little town had its gates closed. No one was in
sight but a man standing on the wall who threatened us
with a lance. So we turned off the road and walked more
or less north, to where I guessed the Oise River to flow.
An intermittent light rain shrouded the world for us.

We didn't mind, we didn't mind anything; Claudia
kept smiling at me in such a radiant way that I had to
stop and kiss her. She shivered like a cat. "I'm very
pleased," she said.

"About what?" I wanted her to say it.

"About having been made a woman, it hurts, I think
it's beautiful, and you belong to me in a way no one
ever has, for I have had you inside myself. So don't look
at me like a cynical student from Paris."

And I stopped looking like a cynical student. The ar-
rogance and the argumentativeness of our university

ideas on love and virginity evaporated from my mind. What we might have proven to be unimportant in our student discussions was important to Claudia, and thus it became important to me.

The concept of her having made love for the first time, and to me, overwhelmed me; and I felt that the answer to that had to be, and was, that I was truly in love, for the first time, with her. I fell into that realization as if it were a warm and voluptuous sea.

Suddenly we started to run; and we continued until we were completely out of breath.

We slept that night under the trees where everything was cold and damp. I was more shy and nervous with her than I had ever been before, but Claudia wasn't shy; she made a kind of lair from her clothes and lay down on it, waiting for me to come and make love to her. There was a soft late light around us, and she looked at me with wide-open clear eyes while I was in her; she had an intensely concentrated, almost puzzled expression on her face, as if she were listening to her own body and what was happening to it with every fiber of her being.

26
. . . .

WE STOOD ON A HILL AND SAW THE OISE RIVER BEFORE US, wide after all the winter and spring rain, and very peaceably winding through green low hills. Clouds of birds were hovering over the fields, and the strong wind carried their cries toward us. Then I heard a rising roar in the air, like carts rattling at great speed over a paved road, or perhaps more like wild water in a stream. And after a while I thought that nothing in nature sounded like this, that it was a human sound. It was the roar one hears in a Paris crowd watching an execution, when the hangman holds up an ear or an arm or a head he has cut off; but from farther away and from a crowd of a size I'd never witnessed. I looked at Claudia and said, "Those are the peasant armies." And in that same moment I saw a group of horsemen ride up to us from very close by; two of them dismounted and very quickly bound our hands behind our backs. I had rehearsed ways to defend myself against something of the kind; now that it happened it went so fast that I didn't even have time to be angry or afraid. And Claudia looked almost as if she had been waiting for this. The group rode on; one of them stayed and led us down the hill toward the river. He didn't speak and he rode quite slowly and without pushing us.

We were brought into an encampment on a flat piece of land bordering the river and sheltered by rows of apple trees. It was part of an abandoned farm. The officer, a dark, bearded young man, was clearly a professional soldier and so were the men around him, about half a dozen of them. And then there were at least twenty or thirty peasants, some fitted out with an odd piece of mail, or armed, but most of them looking as if they'd just come in from their plowing or harvesting. They were eating, sleeping, wrapping their feet in bandages of cloth, or mending their pattens, cleaning a sword or a pike; our arrival didn't arouse their curiosity.

I said that I was a wandering scholar and that Claudia was my wife. "We'll hold you in ransom," the officer said, "unless you want to join us."

"There's no one on earth who'd ransom us," Claudia said immediately and unwisely.

"Then we'll keep you as hostages," the officer said. He beckoned me closer. "We're just a scouting group," he said, "our main body of men is up the valley. Up there things are less, eh, calm. So if you're concerned with your wife's honor, I suggest you join us."

"Why are you on their side?" Claudia said in a loud

prim voice as if she were asking a question in a convent schoolroom.

He smiled at her. "Because, my dear miss—or is it really madam?—they are winning."

Our strangely genteel imprisonment lasted less than a day. Other men started drifting into the camp, peasants who were carrying bags of loot on their backs, with drawn faces, as if they were lugging earth or manure. Some women appeared on the scene too: haggard peasant wives and camp followers in rags with heavy rice powder covering the sores on their faces.

We were locked up in a barn but I could see them mill around. Many of them were getting drunk; I saw couples lying with each other under the trees in full sight of everybody, and shouts and screams were heard from arguments and fist fights over plunder.

I began to call for the officer and when he at last appeared I told him I'd join his troop if he'd free us both immediately. He gave me back the long knife which he had been carrying himself and said we'd have to find our own food. I wondered whether he trusted my decision; he didn't seem to care much one way or the other. "We'll get away," I whispered to Claudia.

That night I sat beside her in the barn. It was crowded there with snoring men and women and the air was heavy with filth and sweat. Our presence seemed already to be taken for granted, but no one had shared his food with us. The handful of regular soldiers had vanished.

Claudia slept but I forced myself to stay awake; I feared for her. Outside the regular cry of the guards was a dull and very unwarlike sound.

At dawn we were attacked.

27

·······

I DON'T KNOW WHAT BECAME OF THE GUARDS WHO HAD BEEN
posted all around the encampment: a raw trumpet note
woke the men in the barn. I had been dozing and hadn't
heard anything either. The peasants rushed out with
their swords and sticks, cursing and pushing. I shook
Claudia. We stayed in the doorway; behind us the
women were cowering in the straw.

This is the sight which awaited us: a line of horsemen
coming down the hillside around us, in a beautiful trot,
the first rays of the sun playing on their helmets and
mail, on the points of their lances and on the pennons and
banners they were carrying. Red and white standards,
shields of blue dappled with golden lilies. "Navarre," I
murmured. Claudia clutched my arm so tightly that I
could feel her nails break the skin. She sighed, "They're
like the knights of God."

And indeed it seemed as if there could be no doubt
about the issues at stake in a battle such as this. The
cavaliers with their shiny lances, on horses caparisoned

in green, purple, black, white, converged on the small, dark, undernourished peasants who were forming a hesitant circle, some of them still desperately yawning and scratching their beards—it seemed as if the forces of light and of darkness were meeting.

There was not even a battle. As the knights reached the flat area of the camp and spurred their horses into a gallop, the peasants broke and ran. A few jumped into the river and drowned or vanished from our sight; others were struck down in flight.

It was all over in a few minutes.

A knight came toward us on foot, his sword drawn; but Claudia ran past him toward the man who was obviously the leader. He wore only light mail and a helmet which he, as he saw her approaching, took off and placed in front of him on his horse. Claudia curtsied to him and kissed his hand. I stood next to her by that time; "We thank you, sir, for delivering us," she said solemnly. He began to laugh; it was the officer who the day before had commanded the peasants.

I looked at Claudia as the peasants who were still alive were bound back to back and flung into the river and the barn was set afire. She paled at the screams of the women in there but then walked off without uttering a word and sat down in the grass a few hundred feet away.

Two of the women in the barn jumped through the flames and ran up the hill; they were not pursued. I don't know how many of them were caught in that barn.

Thick smoke began to rise from the roof and their screaming stopped. Then flames broke through; the wooden structure burned out rapidly; none of the horsemen ever looked that way.

I went over to the officer. "I am Guillaume of Picquigny," he said, "at your service." He and his men were going to follow the river up to the town of Compiègne. I asked his permission for us to come with him; he lent us two horses; mine was the best I'd ever ridden.

28

. . . .

CLAUDIA AND I RODE AT THE TAIL END OF THE COLUMN FOL-
lowing the river bank. Poplars and willows grew down
almost to the water's edge, and often we could see only
the hard colors of the pennons sticking out over the foliage.

Claudia rode in beautiful style. I thought of those ladies
and gentlemen I had watched riding out from Montmélian castle; here I was myself walking a horse in the
green morning beside a noble lady whose scarf I wore. I
grinned; what a splendid adventure, I said to myself,
but very unreal. I tried to think back to the moment
when life had acquired this unreality. Where had it
begun? And why was it difficult now to take this life, to
take anything, even death, quite seriously? Was this the
alchemy of courage? Wasn't Oxford, no, wasn't Aristotle
himself bloodless compared to riding an eager horse, on
a clear day, beside a girl whose lover you were?

That night I slept very deeply. One of those gentlemen
had given us a blanket to roll ourselves in; Claudia crept

in with me so simply and immediately that it gladdened my heart. Such a natural intimacy with her seemed as exciting as the wildest passion.

It was still dark when someone shook me. I opened my eyes and saw one star right above me in the hard black sky; that was the first time on my journey that I needed time to realize where I was, who I was, even.

"Take your horses and walk them to the river," a voice whispered. It was too dark to see who was speaking. "The peasants have laid an ambush ahead. We'll cross the river here, they can't follow us without horses."

I led both our horses; Claudia was drunk with sleep. We mounted in the pitch-dark and stepped down the bank into the water. I held Claudia's horse at the bit, but my own horse stumbled and I had to let go of hers.

I'm no great horseman and had no idea what to do; I let my horse follow its own lead and hoped it would stay with the others. All I could see around me was a vague sheen of light on the smooth surface of the Oise. Its cold water soon rose above my knees; the horse started swimming and I let myself glide out of the saddle and be pulled along. It found its footing again near the other shore with such a shock that I almost let go of the pommel. And then I was standing, dripping, in a marshy field on the west bank of the Oise and sneezed and cursed and called Claudia's name in an undertone.

I found her only when it became light, for her horse had swum farther upstream; when we were all assembled and drying our clothes the absence of Guillaume of Picguigny was noted. "He'll get to us," they said, "a bit of water can't stop Picguigny."

We followed the river in a careful file; the riding was irksome here, for the ground was very soft. At a bend the man ahead reined in with a shout and pointed across the stream. Soon we caught sight of a multitude of men on the other shore; in the virginal early light we could distinguish their rusty helmets and even their beards. When they noticed us, a great cry went up and after considerable pushing the crowd opened as if to show us something.

We saw a willow; from one of its branches dangled a hanged man. Two long strips of cloth, bound around his neck, fluttered like a gay decoration: red and white, the colors of Navarre. "They've hanged Guillaume of Picguigny," our horsemen said.

29

· · · · · · ·

AFTER ANGRY DEBATE OUR COMPANY CHOSE ANOTHER LEAD-
er, a man they called Sir Meles. If Picguigny had been
young, this soldier looked like a child; he was reddish
blond with a little, highly incongruous mustache on his
pink-cheeked face. Someone told me Meles was from
Bohemia. He asked me to join the group; I hesitated and
said, "I'm neither a soldier nor a nobleman." "Arms en-
noble," Meles stated in his guttural French and he
handed me his battle-axe, "since Picguigny seemed to
like you, it's proper you take his place."

I listened to myself; I had never done any real fighting,
and I was curiously waiting for my body or my heart to
give me signals of fear. And to my surprise I felt no fear
at all but smelled the smell of temptation: Sir Meles
tempting me with the easy, the unreal, unserious life.
"I'll join you, at least until Compiègne," I finally said.
"My lady's safety is my first responsibility."

Claudia rode close beside me all that day and she was
highly pleased. "I'll wait for you there, I'll wait in Com-

piègne," she said. "If you are my lover you have to avenge Dammartin for me." As before when we were not alone, she was a different Claudia, a girl I didn't know well at all.

That evening she made me cut her hair with my knife; with her scarf knotted tightly around the waist of her long coat, it made her look like a boy. Later, lying beside me in our blanket, she suddenly told me in a tragic child's whisper that she was so sad about her hair, but I said her boy's cut was pretty and very exciting. She laughed then, and she quivered when I stroked her short hair but she wouldn't allow me even to kiss her, for the others lay too nearby.

There were about twenty of us, with several spare horses, following the right bank of the Oise toward Compiègne. Soon I would see this company fighting again; once more, as when the peasants had been massacred in the river camp, it seemed all too easy. It started when a sharp bend of the river brought a fortified house into view.

"That's Rhuis," they said. "The peasants are holding it. Let's take it."

Nothing further was said; the men rode out in two groups. Meles looked around at me once, and I kicked my horse into a canter. "Fall behind!" I cried to Claudia, but she didn't.

I had a hard time keeping up with them.

The peasants saw us coming, they ran in and closed the

gate, but five or six of them, men and women who had been gathering water and wood, were caught outside. They didn't offer any resistance and Meles had their hands bound; they kept their eyes on the ground without a word, except for one of them.

"We're the king's men," he told us, "the king has escaped from England to lead his people. Don't lift your hand against the king." Meles didn't answer him.

One of the horsemen spat in the peasant's face.

Our prisoners were brought before the gate of the house and Meles shouted at the men inside to surrender. Some of them came out and looked at us from the wall, but they had no archers and were powerless.

A silence fell. It was a sunny day, shortly before noon.

The peasants and the horsemen looked at each other, waiting. And suddenly it all seemed ridiculous. I had the strange feeling that if someone would start laughing, we would all join in; and then we would leave them alone and ride off, while they would simply pick up their scattered wood and start refilling their kicked-over pails.

The hard voice of Meles called four of his riders together. For him time had not been standing still and he sounded impatient. He told them to knot ropes around the wrists and ankles of one of the prisoners, the man who had said not to lift our hand against the king. Horses were pulled up and the ropes tied to the pommels of their saddles.

"Come on," the horsemen cried, almost gaily it seemed,

and clicked their tongues. The prisoner fell to the ground. I focused my eyes on the horse nearest me, a big hackney.

It went all very fast, I saw the horse straining, it didn't know what it was pulling at. The prisoner gave only one single scream. The hackney broke into a trot, dragging part of the quartered body past me.

I couldn't see Claudia anywhere.

The prisoner whose turn it was next screamed for a long time; he had watched the fate of the man before him. Then Meles had ropes bound to the arms and legs of a woman. At that point the gate of Rhuis opened and the peasants came out; there were about three dozen of them. The woman was left lying on the ground.

The peasants put on some display of courage: one of them held a flag with the royal lily, and they cried "Montjoye!" It was almost pathetic; and the knights didn't bother to answer with "Navarre."

Without armor or horses the peasants obviously stood no chance; still one of our company was killed in the melee. I stared in the face of a man who tried to pull me off my horse. He had friendly round cheeks and he was biting his lip; he didn't look into my eyes, he wasn't aware of me as a human being. He was cursing and sweating; "We'll roast you alive," he muttered. I knew they did that; Claudia's father had been lucky, I suddenly thought. I felt numb; as in a dream, all this seemed to take up a long time. But it cannot have been more than a moment. I broke his head with the axe of Sir Meles.

The horsemen let the peasants lie where they had fallen and rode through the gate, taking the women with them. I went to look for Claudia; I found her behind some bushes, bent double, and vomiting desperately.

I wanted to comfort her but she waved me away. I waited nearby until she reappeared, and we went to the house without saying anything to each other about what had happened. When we got there most of the others had already ridden on; it had been decided not to stay in Rhuis. We followed after them. There was no sound or trace of the women.

30
. . . .

AT TWILIGHT WE CAME QUITE UNEXPECTEDLY UPON A VIL-
lage. Without wasting a word the cavaliers spread out
and began cutting down every human being they saw.
A boy ran so close by me that he brushed my leg; one of
the knights wedged him against a hut with his horse
and pulled his dagger. My horse was nervous but I forced
it closer and I lifted the axe. The knight thought that I
wanted to kill the boy; then, when he saw my face, he
tucked the dagger back into his belt and the boy escaped.
The horseman and I stared at each other for a long moment. He shrugged; he turned his horse and while doing
so his eye must have caught the boy again, who was making his way over a field. He went after him and ran him
down with his horse.

"The peasants do the same," Claudia whispered to herself.

We spent the night in that village, emptied of its life,
its chickens eaten, its human beings destroyed. When we

rode off one of the men tried to set fire to it but the wind was too strong and he soon gave up. We rode single file most of the time. Claudia avoided speaking with me or even looking at me.

Compiègne was reached in the afternoon. It was a dead town such as I had never seen, not even as a boy when my mother and I fled to Paris in the year of the great plague. We came upon a closed gate but Sir Meles rode on without hesitation and led us in through a breach in the wall; my horse shied from a pack of dogs tearing away at something or someone beside it. A putrid smell hung heavily in the narrow slippery streets, over which the red and white pennon of Navarre was blowing from the pinnacle of a church. I didn't know what had happened in that town and I did not ask.

I saw soldiers afoot, but their presence did as little to make Compiègne seem more alive as crawling insects do a corpse. They were not its inhabitants but its despoilers. One saw them peer in windows and kick or break in doors when they thought they'd find something they'd fancy; but the plunder must have gone on too long already. The loot they carried out was torn bedding only and heavy furniture which they would discard again before they had gone very far.

"We're too late for the party, gentlemen," Meles said and he laughed. He looked at me, I didn't laugh with him, and he frowned thoughtfully.

In the market square the company scattered. Meles and some of his friends decided to sleep in the guild house which had one of its halls used as a stable; I thought it best to look for shelter in that same building. When I was holding Claudia's horse and mine, Meles rode over in a little trot and suddenly reined in very close to me; I didn't move, which disappointed him. Bending over from the saddle, he took the reins from me. "I'll take these for the moment," he said, "and my axe too. But you can stay under my command." I turned my back on him and entered the building with Claudia. Her hand was hot and dry; she had a fever. I asked her how she felt but she didn't reply. Then I walked her through those endless stone galleries, half carrying her up steep staircases. Finally we found a usable room under the eaves, looking out on the square. "Wait here," I said and hastily went ransacking through other rooms until I had collected enough bedding for her. I also engaged a man to bring us food and wine. Candles were not to be found anywhere; in some halls people sat around by the light of furniture burning in the fireplaces. In those heavily paneled and velvet-draped rooms they still looked what they were, soldiers camping in an open field.

Claudia refused to eat, but I made her drink wine and water all night; only toward dawn did she fall asleep. I felt lightheaded, I'd have given an eye tooth for a talk with a Paris friend, to put things back into some kind of perspective; I wondered what Claudia thought of the fighting we had been in, of avenging Dammartin that way. Then I must have fallen asleep in my seat, for when great shouting from the square woke us, the sun was high in the sky and it was stifling hot in our room.

31

. . . .

NEW FIGHTING HAD BROKEN OUT OVER THE SHELL OF WOOD, stone and mud which was still called Compiègne; some of its inhabitants, with the peasants they had sheltered, had launched an attack from the Forest of Compiègne and were now pouring into the streets through the breaches in the walls.

As I came outside a mob of foot soldiers swept me along with them and carried me beyond the square toward the river. I pushed and kicked my way out of the thick of them and toward a wall where I could breathe and see.

See two swarms of men meet, as red and white termites meet, to kill: to kill with swords and knives, axes, sticks and stones, with nails, feet, and bare hands. Feverish detailed images stood out in the harsh sunlight; a soldier swinging a sword and cutting someone right across his mouth, splitting open his face to the ears; a man kneeling on another and with his knife hastily gouging out one eye, then the other; two men trying to strangle each other, with glazed eyes, purple faces. And all were sweating, I know not with the heat of the day or with the fear of death, and all looked so alike in this blind shuffle at the edge of life that I did not know how friend and enemy were distinguished.

Hands clawed at my leg: a wounded man was lying in the gutter, clutching a knife and attempting to drag me down. I tried to shake loose but couldn't; then I kicked him in his face. I felt and heard it give in under the weight of my boot, and I fled from that awful sound.

I turned into an alley but came upon a blind wall and leaned against it, exhausted. It was so narrow that only a ribbon of sky shone over my head; its entrance which must have faced toward the river was a brightly glittering oblong of light. Then a shadow filled it: two men entered the alley and stood still when they saw me. They were armed with sticks only, they looked like peasants; their bearded faces were dark and dirty and their eyes looked frightened. They came toward me, one behind the other; I pulled my knife and said in a hoarse voice, "You fools, how do you know who I am?" They did not stop; the one in front lunged at me and hit me on the hand with his stick, and I dropped my knife. He jumped, we fell together, and my hand closed on my knife again as I hit the mud and I stabbed him in the side. I got back on my feet, tearing my cheek on the molded cold stone of the wall as I did; the other man turned and ran, I caught up with him at the beginning of the alley and plunged my knife into the low of his back. I let go of it and thought vaguely, why did I do that, who can give me forgiveness for that, and jumping over the dying and the wounded lying on the now abandoned riverside I ran to the market square. I don't know where the fighting had moved to; the square was empty, in the entrance hall of the guild house a servant was holding two horses. Claudia wasn't in the room under the eaves; I found her in the courtyard, burning with fever, her lips parched and bruised and her dress torn; I cried had she been molested but she just closed her eyes. I dragged her to the entrance hall and made the servant help me hoist her onto one of the horses. "But who are you?" he suddenly shouted, laying a hand on my arm. I still had my short knife, I stabbed him in his shoulder and he fell to the floor with a loud wail; I climbed onto the horse behind Claudia and rode out into the square, stumbling but holding on, steering the horse away from where I heard screaming and banging, and hardly daring to breathe until we were out under the trees of the forest.

32

. . . .

CLAUDIA WAS DELIRIOUS FOR SEVERAL DAYS, AND THAT TIME, far from being anxious, was restorative. As soon as we were out of the town I felt master of my fate again. I never doubted her recovery—for even in her violent fever she looked unshakeably firm and young and of this earth—and with her mind following the far paths of her fever dreams, I was more alone with her true self than I had ever been.

That aloneness with her healed me. It erased what had come between us, my jealousy of Robert of Lorris and the almost imperceptible sting hidden, because of that, in her sudden giving herself; her ideas of chivalry and revenge; the awareness of another Claudia; and the blood and violence in which all that had been bathed.

Attending her, I was taken back to the innocence of our first morning on the lawn of Dammartin; but now it was a knowing innocence.

I rode her to Ermenonville in one wild journey and found Robert of Lorris' house open to us. Neither he nor his father was there but the major-domo immediately recognized Claudia and gave us without question the best room in the establishment; apart from him only a few servants had stayed at their posts. The weather was hot, the house lay cool, quiet and as if forgotten in its park. There was food, and a woman who brought Claudia pots of herb tea at all hours.

I sat by her bedside, I studied her pale lovely face.

One day she woke up and looked at me with clear eyes; her fever was gone. We stared at each other without saying a word.

I knelt near her and kissed her, and she put her hand on my neck and held my face against hers.

33
· · · · · · ·

AND I THOUGHT BACK TO THE MORNING WHEN THE HORSE-
men with the shining lances had come trotting down the
hillside in the growing sunlight and destroyed the
peasants.

The green hours when I was riding beside Claudia
along the river at the tail end of a many-colored column
and felt that nothing mattered in life, neither learning
nor death, only this keen joy of being alive in one's body
totally without fear, acknowledging the beauty of
attack: running toward a man in battle to kill him, falling on a woman in making love.

I thought, I am glad I have believed and felt this once;
it is false but only someone who has gone through the
believing may bear witness to its falsehood. Only he
knows that it's neither baseness nor cowardice which
makes him a witness against it, but his very reality as a
human being. I have been a knight and a nobleman during those few hours, and therefore I can now renounce
knighthood; I can be a man in a nobler way.

Perhaps the miserable serfs who waited so long before rising with sticks and stones against the horsemen in silver mail are the truer knights of France, closer to the knighthood of Christ who could not kill. On each side death is darkness and justice light.

I must talk about this with Claudia to make her regain her faith; but then she might laugh and call me a student and a priest, or be a tigress, believing that I'm condoning the murder of her father and the destruction of her house.

But Claudia did not speak about avenging Dammartin, and she liked calling me "student" now, saying the word in a caressing way.

34
· · · · · · ·

SHE WAS VERY WEAK, I WAS BATTERED TOO, AND WE WERE both exhausted, bruised all over, with feet still so sore that they refused to go into our boots. The need to heal prevented us from feeling guilty for those white silent days in Ermenonville. In the long evenings we went to bed at sunset.

When Claudia's fever had gone she told me very briskly that I could now sleep with her in the bed instead of on my bench under the window. And so I came to lie beside her and looked at her, feeling rather foolish; she laughed and said, "You can kiss me, you won't catch my fever."

"I wasn't afraid of that. I thought—"

"I want you to kiss me. I've dreamt of it. It must have made the fever worse."

She made me undress her; it was the first time we were like that in a real bed together. Then she pulled the bed-clothes away and stated, "You must know, Heron, that I've never seen a naked man in my life." My breath caught in my throat, I didn't know what to answer; finally I managed to say, "Well, perhaps you'd better see this one then."

We made love as I don't think I ever had before; and of a sudden I saw Claudia's eyes break, and she gasped as if stabbed with a knife. She lay still for a long time with her eyes closed and then she whispered, "I've never felt anything like that—is that how love-making is? Is that what happens to a girl?"

But then she began to cry, "I have sinned," she murmured, "this must be what I read once, and didn't understand, about the incubi and succubi."

I kissed her on her eyes and said that she hadn't sinned, that she was learning about love as God had meant her to when He made her beautiful; that it was a divine emotion and that the Greeks had their special goddess for it, Venus, Aphrodite.

"You're a heathen," she said, and smiled again.

"No, it's not heathenish, we learned this from the priests at the university."

"I don't believe it," she said.

It had grown dark in the room.

"I'll tell you a story," I said. "Be careful with it, it must be dangerous, I was thrown out of my college for it. But I'd written it as a poem for myself and I hadn't meant anyone to read it.

"I don't really believe the world was created in seven days, I don't think many scholars do either although they won't say it. But the world must have been created bit by bit, beginning with sky and earth and other dead things, all alone in a dead universe, a huge lifeless machine.

"And then animals and men were created, and there was movement in the world not directly governed by God. But still, this movement wasn't so different from a running stream or the circling sun because there was no emotion in it.

"And then there was the first orgasm in the universe."

"What is that?" Claudia asked.

"That's what my poem is about. That's . . . that's the word for what happened. They had words for those things in the pagan world and talked about them. My poem says that the first orgasm, I don't know whether it was of a man and a woman or of animals, was the first emotional movement in the world, the birth of love, and the beginning of creation."

35

. . . .

IN PRINCIPIO ERAT VERBUM, ET VERBUM ERAT APUD DEUM,
et Deus erat verbum; in the beginning was the word, and
the word was with God and the word was God. I thought
that it didn't sound better in Latin, this Latin sounded
like words on the pots of an apothecary. I wished I could
read it in Greek.

For I had the feeling that I suddenly understood it.
And I tried to tell Claudia that I no longer believed in my
poem, how creation began in the first orgasm in the
universe. For without words emotion must have been
blind; through words only, and not before, emotion and
love could become seeing.

Before loving someone, you had to say that you loved
her, speaking to her or even to yourself. Before being able
to love you had to be able to speak the words. You needed
the will to say them, the will to sacrifice and negate yourself.

Where could such a will come from, she asked.

From being lost in the higher beauty of a woman, from the mystical intoxication of a girl's body, her eyes, her smile.

THE GARDEN OF ERMENONVILLE HAD GROWN WILD. THERE were still traces of its rose beds and clipped hedges, but all was invaded by grasses and weeds. Wild flowers grew everywhere and the sharp herb smell penetrated to our room; it softened the inexorableness of those hard stone walls and stairwells surrounding us. Perhaps we deserved this time in our worldly monastery because we never questioned its miraculous and God-given quality. The major-domo asked us when his masters would return to Ermenonville; we told him: soon, for he looked as if that were the answer he hoped for and needed. He left us after that, but he had brought the world and the fighting back with us. "When my father was sick with the plague ten years ago," I told Claudia, "in the town of Valenciennes, my mother nursed him, and I helped. Everyone was sick, or fled, husbands from wives, parents from children. But she stayed with him and nursed him, though he died. And I swore to myself that I'd try to act like her one day."

I didn't think Claudia was listening but I had to say this, for myself: "Now the people are suffering from a plague which wants no nursing. This is a plague really to flee from.

"I know you wanted me to avenge Dammartin and I'd listened to enough ballads to make me believe that I should. I broke a man's head, and killed two others with my knife. You are my lady, but I no longer think that Dammartin was an outrage against you, I think it was one blow in an endless senseless battle men are waging against each other. I want to be free from that battle; and not out of fear."

Claudia didn't answer.

"You don't think I'm afraid, do you?" I asked.

She shook her head. Then she said in an undertone, "But one has to take sides—"

"If I were a giant I'd fight both sides."

"I know about that endless battle," Claudia said, "but why are the peasants in it? They never were."

" 'To destroy the world,' the abbot said, and I believe him. But the world tried to destroy them first, and perhaps that world has to be destroyed. When I walked out of Paris first I felt as if even the fields were waiting for death and rebirth. Perhaps men feel the same now, deep in their souls, unknowingly; our generation was born nostalgic for what they've never known, and that's why they kill."

"You told me in our garden that you wanted to be free

so much," Claudia said. "Now I want to be free too. But how do we know we have the right to?"

"Oh of course we have!" I cried. "For you'll see, it's much much harder to be free than to take sides."

"And if you wanted to be free so much, aren't you regretting that you didn't sail to England before, when you could?" she asked.

"No, because I will again and with you, I hoped for it that way. I want to be free with you, not alone."

"I do too," Claudia said rapidly, "for love's sake. I want my hour of love and then they can come and murder me also."

I kissed her and said that she would have many hours, and that no one would touch a hair on her head.

But in the night I woke, I peered at the contour of her face, her closed eyes, beside me, and I feared for her. The horse on which we had come was still there, the only one left in the stables of Robert's house; it was fat with grazing and it had lost its shoes but it could carry me to the village nearby. I left long before dawn, without waking Claudia, in the false light of a waning moon. The village had a priest who would know what was happening.

He told me that the peasants held all the castles of Ile de France. "But the French and the English have united, with Navarre, against them," he said indifferently, "those enemies have united after twenty years, to crush the serfs of France."

He walked a few steps away, then turned to me once

more, hesitating. And his heavy and flaccid face had changed startlingly; he looked stern and in pain. He added, "The rulers have destroyed the hope of the people. They rule with a rod of iron; and as the vessel of a potter shall the people be broken to smithers—thus said Saint John."

I didn't tell Claudia where I had been. I repeated her words to me, "I want my hour."

AND SO, NOT IN SPITE BUT BECAUSE OF THE WAR, WE thought of love.

We loved each other, and better than Tristan and Iseult, without any coyness, for a hard light of passion had been lit in Claudia.

I didn't serve her like the knight of the "pure love" who must prove his servitude by not giving in to his desire. What love is that? Only a man, and a dull one, could have thought it up. Claudia was served because the fulfillment of her desire was more important than the fulfillment of my own. Lying beside her I felt like a slave looking up at a goddess; she was, or seemed to me, incomparably beautiful then. Even just touching her body seemed unthinkable unless it were done to give her pleasure rather than to use her in taking pleasure.

She was indeed, as the poet Catullus had written of Claudia Pulcher, "loved by us both." Her body became our temple, we discussed her thighs, her curves, her shoulders as if she were architecture. She was shy in taking off the most innocent garment, in showing me her ankle; and from that state we fell, each time, into sudden wild unbelievable intimacies in which I caressed her, kissed her belly, in which she took me between her breasts and even in her mouth. We had never heard of such things; once as we were sitting in the grass against a hedge she must have been thinking of them; she paled and said, "Ours is an unforgivable sin."

I denied it; she asked in an undertone, "Can you prove it isn't so?"

It was a sunny morning; I could hear the voices of servants behind the hedge. But I gently pushed her down into the grass and took off her clothes, and started kissing her slowly, from her feet up along her legs, and came to her, in a very hard rhythm; she bit her lip and then I went out of her. I leaned over her and said, "Say it was no sin, and I'll come back." She turned her head and bit my hand so fiercely that it started bleeding hard; she didn't bite in passion but in black fury. "Come back," she whispered.

Later she said, "I didn't say it was no sin. I don't know."

"The priest in the village will marry us," I said.

She shook her head. "I don't want to defy fate even more."

38

· · · · · · ·

CLAUDIA FOUND GREEN DYE IN THE HOUSE AND STARTED knitting me a scarf in green wool; "red life, white death, green grave," I said.

"Oh no, not that, green is the color of passion." She looked at me with narrow narrow eyes; they were almost pure grey. "I feel passion for you," she said. "I will eat you."

"You may," I answered.

The war, the very land beyond Ermenonville, became like a strange dream. "I know many people are dead," she said. "I haven't forgotten. But *we're* not dead."

One day we walked farther than we had before, and we found a stream which ran between steep high banks covered with mulberry bushes almost touching each other. There was a kind of step in one of the banks; I let myself glide down to it and Claudia followed me. We sat with our feet dangling and our arms around each other; the air was warm and sweet; the bushes made a green cupola over our heads.

We caressed each other; "Shall we be together, or I first?" Claudia said softly, "I am very close."

I began to laugh afterward, just from being happy; "You know everything now," I said to her, "and you're a very brazen girl. Were you really innocent when I met you?"

She began to laugh too. "I'm still innocent," she said, "innocent for both of us. You are me."

And when we were lying silently in each other's arms against the warm earth of the bank of the stream, it seemed indeed to be so, that I was her, and she me. The air and the green-filtered light were motionless, we were in a hollow of utter quiet. We lay beneath the surface of the earth, life had closed over us, we were unborn, beyond death, and that same oneness found in the hurtingly short moment of bursting loose in her now enveloped us generously, without ending.

When we walked back to the house in the evening, Claudia said, "If I ever complain in the future, I want you to remind me of what I say now: I had my hour." And I said: "And I, my freedom."

When we neared the gate we saw a great commotion around the house. Robert of Lorris had returned.

39
· · · · · · ·

SURPRISINGLY, WE ALL EMBRACED AS IF WE HAD SEPARATED
on the best of terms. I was truly glad to see Robert of
Lorris back: jealousy had become unthinkable. And
there was a kind of blissfulness about Claudia and me
which we wanted to pour out over the heads of others—
for a moment we felt as if Robert had come back to be
converted by us, to hear about love.

"I didn't go to join my father, Claudia," he told her
very seriously.

"We're glad you left the fighting," she said, "whatever side it was on."

"I was on my own side only. I rode to Clermont to try
and get my father released. Charles of Navarre himself,
with some of his cavalry, met an army of peasants at
Clermont in Beauvoisis. There were negotiations for a
truce; the peasants sent Guillame Caillet and my father
as parliamentarians. Caillet was hanged from the battle-
ments by Navarre: no one knows where my father is.
When the news reached us, I went to Clermont with a

thousand deniers in gold, all we have, to ransom him. But Charles had withdrawn, Clermont stands empty, and the forest of Hez is thick with dead peasants, three thousand of them, they say. I saw—" He looked at Claudia and fell silent.

"The tide has turned," Robert said, without any emotion in his voice. "The king has not left his English prison, and the French knights are not fighting with their serfs but against them."

He looked at us. "You'll be safe here for a while. All of Ile de France from the Oise to beyond the Marne is still solidly in the hands of the people, and Jean Vaillant has come out of Paris with two thousand men to help them. You'll be forewarned before vengeance descends on this house." These last words he said ironically.

Claudia wandered over to the window and looked out into the darkening park.

"A truce of God has to be declared," I said to him. "They can't kill off the peasants. Who would feed the world?"

He answered, "I thought of that when I saw what they had done to the villages and fields around Clermont. But they don't draw the connection. This has become a war like no war I ever heard of. They don't look upon the people—and my father," he added after a pause—"as enemies, they look upon them as a disease."

After a while I said, "I'm grateful for your hospitality, and for your safe return."

"You have changed very much, Claudia and you," he said almost wistfully. "I've known Claudia since she was a little child. How she has changed! You have consoled her too—no, disembittered her. I'd like to be your friend for that."

I bowed.

"I will stay here," he said, "but you must take Claudia away if I tell you to; I wouldn't know where, but we'll find a way out. Give me your promise you'll protect her."

"I don't have to promise you, nor myself," I answered, "for it couldn't be otherwise."

"Poor Robert," Claudia said when she lay with her head on my shoulder in our deep bed in the dark room; and I knew what she meant with those words. I buried my mouth in her soft short hair, and kissing her was like saying a prayer.

40

. . . .

TWO MEN FROM THE ESTATE CAME BACK TO IT AND BEGGED Robert of Lorris for shelter. They were on foot and in rags; they had escaped from a battle in the town of Meaux. I'm certain he put them somewhere, but we never saw them again. I came upon Robert in the park; then he told me about Meaux.

Meaux on the river Marne was one of the towns through which the peasants' rising had changed substance as leaven changes the dough of bread. In the lighter air of the town, where a man can lift his eyes from the earth and look up, the brutish resistance of cornered animals had become a thinking act. The citizens of Meaux opened their gates to a peasant army adopting the banner of its absent king, and to the men who had come from Paris to join them. There were thousands of them, ten thousand, Robert said. Meaux had a market building away from the heart of town and almost completely surrounded by the river; here scores of gentlemen and their families had taken refuge when their houses were burned by their serfs. The peasants entering Meaux did not attack them; since the market was cut off from the outside world, the aristocrats inside became virtually their hostages.

In that town, perhaps for the first time, a mood of something akin to complaisance took hold. Victors can afford such a mood; but the peasant army in Meaux could not.

It was a Saturday morning.

The people of Meaux brought trestle tables out into the streets and served the army meat, bread and wine. The men were sitting in long rows in the green shadow under the trees, eating and drinking. The air was cool and luminous; it was more like a country fair than a scene of war. But, Robert had been told, the peasants didn't behave like peasants; they didn't get drunk and they didn't curse and fight over the food. They were oddly restrained, they looked at the men who had come from Paris and they imitated their way of eating. They felt they had suddenly become soldiers and free men, and tried to rise to the occasion. In the square stood a guard holding a blue standard with the three golden lilies of the absent king.

A man came running and said that he'd seen horsemen approaching the town from the east. The word spread along the tables. The talking ceased, and then a few, soon followed by all, flocked out into the square. The children started running around the abandoned tables and stealing the food.

Early that morning, a Gascon, the Lord of Buch, leading a company of several hundred knights down the valley of the Marne, was informed by a traveling merchant of the entrance of an army of peasants into Meaux. Buch was on his way home, Gascony, from East Prussia. In that country, east of the river Oder, live Slav tribes who have not been converted. Raiding those heathens is good sport, and Buch had been at it for several months. He and his company had killed at least ten thousand Slavs and the news had reached France of the considerable booty of leather and furs they had amassed; women too, but these had been left behind. They had started back in high spirits, these knights, but for the past few days they had heard disquieting reports about the peasants of northern France.

Buch decided to attack the peasants in Meaux.

The lowly people of Ile de France had started their war with nothing but despair. They had no arms, no horses, no discipline, and although manual labor had made them hard, with their undernourished bodies they were no match for well-trained gentlemen. They had nothing to lose, and thus they had begun by winning; then success had given them self-confidence and a measure of discipline. But their success had always been based on overwhelming superiority of numbers. They were no

129

cowards; surprisingly enough they had shown spirit and self-sacrifice. When a mounted knight attacked these men, all they could do was choke him in their own flesh; five or ten had to give their lives before the knight was subdued. They fought the way a pack of dogs fights a wolf or a boar, the way ants bridge a rivulet.

Such fighting was not possible within the confinement of streets; the strange fortunes of war, though, now provided them with a town that was on their side. If these peasants had fought in the streets of Meaux in the manner of bandits or cutthroats, from doorways and windows, retreating and coming back, making use of each house and each obstacle, they might have held their own against the knights of Buch. But they had been received in that town like soldiers; citizens of Meaux and Paris had sat and eaten with them. They did not think of withdrawals or tricks; they made front on the river bridge facing east. They stood there bravely; and doing so they couldn't even deploy and gain the advantage of their numbers.

When the horsemen of Buch rode down toward that river they must have had that pleasant tingle in their stomachs they hadn't felt since Prussia. They were going hunting, and men were their game. They closed their visors and with that simple gesture they became invulnerable as far as the peasants were concerned.

Buch cut through the peasants like a sickle through the grass. Each of his men cut his path like a harvester;

the peasants were the harvest. Two or three knights were pulled off their horses and killed, but their killers were immediately run under foot. Soon the peasants tried to flee, but there was no escape except drowning in the river. The knights became drunk with blood; never was human flesh set upon with such fire and such contempt.

When it was all over, Buch's company assembled, the horses gingerly picking their way through and over the bodies. The old town was set afire by the knights and they waited, like hunters in a battue, to kill whoever escaped from the flames. Finally the smoke, the stench of burning flesh and their exhausted sword arms made them decide they'd had enough.

It was midafternoon as they rode on, followed at a distance by the gentry from the market building. The weather had turned sultry. Behind them, under the low heavy sky, Meaux did not burn well; its roofs smoldered and the smoke hung wet in the bloody streets.

The men and the women of the army and the town who had somehow escaped, a few hundred, drifted into Valois and into Champagne across the river, carrying with them the story of the defeat. In the other direction, converging on the smell of the ten thousand abandoned bodies, wandered, flew, crawled wolves, dogs, crows, ravens, insects: the last inhabitants of Meaux.

41
....

IT WAS NOW EARLY SUMMER, JUNE, WITH QUICK WHISPER-
ing nights and warm days; dawns in which Claudia and
I got up and out of the house, without seeing anyone, and
walked in the grass in our bare feet. I had never before
been so aware of each sound, each touch, everything I
looked at, each passing minute.

We hardly saw Robert. He had kept himself apart
since his return, whether to protect his own privacy or to
respect ours, I did not know. He had come back looking
drawn and thin, but he was so young that it didn't make
him seem older; it gave him the appearance of a fierce
sick child. Claudia and I had said to each other that we
would help him and make him feel less lonely. Yet the
days went by without us talking to him: time seemed so
desperately short and precious.

I tried to console myself by thinking: if you love someone, you live within your own calendar and you aren't
able to foresee a termination, you shouldn't be. But when
I told this to Claudia, she answered, "I think that perhaps

you can only be in love when you're aware of an end to it."

"Claudia!" I cried.

"I'm not being morose," she said. "My father used to say, death will be the last remedy."

She caught her breath and listened to the echo of her own words which had frightened her. Then she smiled hesitantly. "If we go to Heaven I'll meet you there," she said.

I embraced her and she started to cry; "You mustn't cry, you mustn't," I whispered, "once you've loved somebody you've broken through your loneliness, you can never be lonely again, that's what love is for—"

But I felt as if a veil were drawn over my eyes, blacking out the world. The thought that the earth was just a passing stage, that we must leave it with our dream unfulfilled, that we would indeed have no more than the brief hour which we had said was all we wanted—that thought seemed so saddening that it was literally unbearable, and I banned it from my mind.

Claudia gave me a piece of paper which had a sentence in Latin written on it.

"What is it?" I asked.

"I bought it from a gypsy. She had a box full. She said it was about my future."

"Do you know what it means?"

"Yes, but tell me."

I knew those words well; they were the twenty-eighth

verse of the second chapter of Saint John's Revelation. The schoolmen of Paris would have been pleased with me.

"And I shall give her," I translated (it said: him, but I read: her), "and I shall give her the morning star."

IN THE END THE ATTACK ON ERMENONVILLE HOUSE CAME
unexpectedly. I don't know who carried the warning to
Robert. It was a late afternoon; half a dozen troopers had
been sighted who might and might not be aiming for us.
The only large window in that house was in the hall; the
servants hastily boarded it up with the heavy oaken and
iron shutters. "Don't be alarmed," Robert said, "this
place can be held against more than six. But I want you
to leave after nightfall."

"We won't," Claudia said.

Ermenonville House had no moat or free outer walls;
it was a simple manor house, facing east, one oblong
structure with first the kitchens, then the pantry, then
the large hall and as an end piece the solar, with three
rooms and the cellars, at a right angle to the rest of the
house. The hall gave onto the park through a square
vestibule; little roundheaded windows ran high along
the walls and through these the approaches could be cov-

ered. The entrance hall jutted out on three sides; it had a flat roof with a parapet around it. To get onto it you had to crawl through a trap door. That night the three of us slept together in the hall. In all, there were six servants left still young enough, or grown up enough, to be of use, and two of them could work a cross-bow.

With the first light Robert and I crept out onto the roof. There was a taste to the air, it tasted of spring water. Around us, fields and woods lay in deadly silence. Woolen rolls of mist were draped over the landscape. Then a solitary cock crowed from quite far away; the sound carried sharply across the silence. "That one's been lucky," Robert muttered.

"So far he's escaped many pots," I said.

"French pots, English pots, Navarran pots, peasant pots—"

"A brave bird!"

"Or a neutral bird."

We began to smile at each other.

And for that moment Robert came back from that strange exile he had sent himself into. He put his arm around my shoulder and sighed, "Oh Lord, oh Lord." We stood like that, peering out over the empty landscape.

A man rode out from under the trees; we had expected someone but a shock went through me all the same. Robert took his arm away and I was ashamed and wondered for a moment whether he thought I was afraid.

The man was holding up a stick with a strip of white

cloth bound to it; he came up to the house, looking around uneasily. He hadn't seen us yet.

"What do you want?" Robert cried.

The man started, then he took off his beret and bowed in the saddle. "On behalf of Navarre," he called at us, "we have come to make Robert of Lorris a prisoner and to redeem his hostages. If he gives himself up his house will remain unmolested."

Robert seemed to ponder his answer.

"Which hostages?" I asked him in great surprise.

He smiled. "They must be thinking of Claudia and you."

I wanted to step up on a crenel but he held me back. "Wait," he said, "perhaps it's the best way out for you two to play that game."

I shook my head without speaking.

"Think of Claudia then," he said.

"She would not want it," I told him, and got up on the stone. "Which hostages?" I cried to the man below.

He looked at me dubiously; he was very afraid of some trap. "The Saint-Jean lady and her cousin," he said.

"I'm the cousin, and I speak too for Claudia de Saint-Jean. We're no hostages. We're friends of Robert of Lorris, we stand beside him, we defy the lot of you. Go to hell! And don't look so scared, you'll wet your pants."

The man wheeled his horse around. "You just put a noose around your own neck too," he shouted at me, riding away.

I was so angry, I almost fell off the parapet. "Go find yourself an old peasant to fight!" I shouted back after him, "Go lance a cow, sir knight!"

"You're mad," Robert said, but he looked very happy.

Eight, not five, troopers joined the courier at the edge of the wood. We could see them argue; it was as if the motionless morning air would carry their very words all the way to our post.

Finally they split into two groups and surrounded the house at a distance. "They don't know what to do," Robert said.

One of these men had a bundle of sticks, as used in building ramparts, behind his saddle; we saw him set fire to it and then he trotted up to the house and threw it against the entrance gate in passing. A futile thing to do: soon the wind got hold of the burning sticks and blew them all across the grass. At that point Claudia opened the trap door but Robert sharply ordered her back.

After a long wait another man rode past the house; one of our servants took a shot at this one and hit his horse. "Simon did that," Robert said. "Bravo for Simon," I answered.

Robert said it wasn't proper to hit a horse; I told him he was out of his mind. The soldier dismounted and led the stumbling horse out of sight.

In the late afternoon the group broke up and rode off.

But the following morning they were back; now there were thirty or more of them, and they had brought mantlets: huge shields, and a tree trunk for use as a battering ram. We were wakened by the sound of that tree banging against the entrance gate, its blows echoing through the house with a dull reverberation.

43

......

THERE WASN'T A CHANCE TO HOLD THE HOUSE AGAINST THIS force. Back to the roof we went, and Robert called for their captain. Covering himself behind the parapet, he asked if yesterday's conditions still held.

"Yes, you coward," the captain cried.

"Will you fight me if I come out?" Robert shouted back, with a frightening catch in his voice.

"I cannot; your father resigned his rank, you're not a knight but a renegade. I won't fight you."

Robert grew pale, but he half turned and smiled at me. "Let's go in and think," he said.

The troop had stopped their battering. The door looked as if it wouldn't last much longer.

"I'm going to give myself up," Robert said to us. "Tell them you were hostages after all."

Claudia started to cry; she looked suddenly worn and tired and like a girl of twelve.

I was furious, "Don't be a fool," I whispered to Robert, "they'll kill you, and burn down the house on top of us.

Let's make a break for it from the cellar window, or from somewhere."

He made an ironical face. He was so alone and withdrawn then, it was as if my words didn't reach him. "I have a better idea," he said, "I'll show you."

We climbed out onto the roof. Robert stepped up on a crenel and drew his dagger from his belt. "Captain," he shouted. I tried to pull him back down but he struck my hand away sharply with the blade. The captain rode out to us and looked up.

"Have you made up your mind, Robert?" he asked.

I realized then that these two knew each other.

"Yes!" Robert answered, and with that cry he jumped down, landed on his feet beside the other and stabbed him in his stomach under his mail jacket; so fast that the cry "yes" still seemed to vibrate in the air as the captain tumbled off his horse and Robert vanished from my sight under three or four soldiers who fell on him with their swords and daggers.

I went back in blindly, the servants had vanished, there was no one left in the hall but Claudia. "He has given himself up," I heard myself say, "but they will not spare this house." And it is too late, I added without making a sound, it is too late in all eternity for us to talk with Robert of Lorris as we had meant to so much, too late to cheer him up, too late to give him anything.

I took Claudia's hand. We ran and jumped down the stone steps to the cellar.

I crouched under its porthole, lifted Claudia and made her crawl through. "There's no one out here," she called softly. The battering on the entrance door began anew. I rolled a barrel in place and got my hands on the stone ledge, I pushed and she pulled, my jacket tore and my skin was chafed off along the whole length of my back. The hellish pain from that I felt only later. I got out, we ran, bending low, to the trees. At the edge of the wood I looked around once and saw two men ride after us. "To the stream," I said.

I think she had more strength than I that morning; at times we dragged each other. There were shouts and the clop of horses behind us, but we reached our stream and let ourselves fall right through those bushes.

And all that day we hid there against the bank, the cold water from the hills running over our feet. We heard voices, seemingly from all directions, and then silence fell, and a sharp smell of smoke reached us. "It's the house," Claudia whispered.

44

· · · · · · ·

WHEN IT BECAME DARK WE CLIMBED OUT OF OUR HIDING
place with great difficulty: my back had become so stiff
and sore that I could hardly move. Claudia took my
jacket off for me; my blouse was stuck against the raw
skin and she had to tear it loose with quick pulls. I
rolled it up and bound it around my waist.

It was cold and dank under the trees. We stood there,
shivering and listening, but the only sound was that of
the wind in the leaves. Neither of us wanted to speak
first. "They murdered Robert," I finally tried to say, but
the words came out inaudibly and I had to repeat them,
hoarsely, "they murdered Robert and I want to do something—" Claudia looked up at me; her pale face caught
the diffused light of the wood. "If you kill a knight you'll
be avenging Robert," she said, "and if you kill a peasant,
Dammartin." "Let's kill them all then," I said, "for they
now all want to kill us; you can see being free isn't so
easy." "Let's find some shelter," she answered, putting
her hands softly against my chest for a moment.

I don't know which direction we walked that night, or why. Going through the brushwood and along the low slopes, I saw us as walking over the earth without finding a place, without finding someone who'd make room for us; we were lost, in an absolute sense.

We came to a circle of trees, thick moss growing underfoot. We rested there, Claudia leaning against a tree, I lying prone and still stripped to the waist. Then, for the only time, I had to fight back an outburst of misery and despair. "We'll manage," I said to myself, and "It doesn't matter. What will happen, will happen."

I heard the sharp ticking of raindrops begin in the foliage, hesitatingly, then faster, then stopping again. A fox barked, owls screeched suddenly right by us. Claudia took my hand without saying anything.

I got up; I was so bruised and sore that I had to do it in stages. "I'll make a fire," I said, "we can't go any farther."

"They might see us."

"Let 'em."

I stumbled around, collecting branches and dead leaves by touch rather than by sight. All was damp; I piled them in Claudia's lap and she tried to dry them on her dress. I dug in the ground under the top layer for dry moss and came back with some handfuls. I had a piece of flint in my pocket; I struck away at it with the blade of my knife as hard as I could. It sparked, and some of the sparks fell where I wanted them to, but nothing happened. Claudia lay down on her stomach next to me and blew on the moss, but without any effect. Then I unrolled my blouse and tore off narrow strips; with these and the moss we built a little pile. A spark set it smoldering for a moment but it went out again, another one, and out again. Then some threads in the linen started to glow. And just when the ticking of the rain in the leaves began anew, a little tongue of flame jumped up and our fire caught.

Claudia dozed through that night, half propped up against the roots of a tree; I shifted around rather helplessly from one side onto the other. Every now and again a gush of rain would descend on us; but our little fire now burned steadily within a ring of branches which took their turn in drying, sheltered by my blouse stretched over a couple of sticks.

The flames had divided the gloom around us into two: a jumping circle of light and impenetrable darkness beyond it. As the flames rose and subsided, the circle grew and contracted; the darkness advanced and retreated again. It was a wild, unknown, unknowing darkness, filled with the cries of animals and ghosts, with Robert's "yes!"; and I thought that our light circle was like life itself, and the border of the black untamed night was like death, like the border of the earth.

When a first hint of greyness seeped into the sky, the

drizzle stopped, and Claudia fell into a deep sleep. I very carefully put my head down in her lap, and I fell asleep too.

45
. . . .

IN THE MORNING THE WIND ROSE AND A DRIVING RAIN SWEPT across the flat lands of Valois. Claudia woke up, hesitated between crying and smiling, and smiled. I lay on my stomach in the moss and looked at her. "The water is lovely and cool on my back," I said, "I like the rain."

She shivered, and we decided to walk on. Everything we wore, everything around us was wet, but we were soon warm for the air was mild. Low clouds swept across the sky, there was a continuous sound of ticking, dripping, rushing water; crows and ravens flew cawing just over the tops of the trees.

"Tilt your face upward while you walk," Claudia said.

"Why?"

"I'm doing it, it feels good. It feels—the rain is washing away the salt of all the tears I ever cried."

"If I weren't in love with you, Claudia," I said, "I'd fall in love with you now because you said that."

She turned toward me, all shiny with rain.

"I want to kiss you," I said.

"I'd blow bubbles, like a fish."

There was a clap of thunder very near us and with that the rainstorm was suddenly over and blue patches of sky appeared.

46
· · · · · · ·

SUNLIGHT FLOODED THE WORLD AS WE WALKED NORTH
through the wood. "You're getting a beautiful scab on
your back," Claudia said, touching me with her finger-
nails, "when it's healed underneath I want to pick it off."
"Don't be so disgusting," I said, and we laughed.

"Why are we laughing?" she asked.

"I don't know. I really don't know. Things could
hardly be worse."

"Perhaps that's why. Nothing can hurt us any more."

"You're a very brave girl," I said.

"No, I'm not being brave." And after a while she
added, "You know what? I know it sounds wild, but I'm
happy."

The soil under our feet became sandier; the moss
stopped. The white sand reflected the bright light filter-
ing through the trees; we left the beeches and elms behind us and came into a pine forest. Then we saw a pond;
I swept the duckweed aside and we drank from the hol-
lows of our hands, Claudia with her mouth puckered,

and shivering because of the little slimy things we felt glide down our throats.

We lay down on the sand with a sigh. "Now make love to me," Claudia said.

"I'm too hungry, I can't."

"Oh yes you can, I'll show you."

She put off her clothes and stood before me.

"You've become an even greater beauty than you were that evening in Crépy," I said to her, in amazement almost.

She laughed, very pleased, and wheeled around, suddenly became shy and lay down with closed eyes. We made love, as she had said we would, and being with Claudia, lying on her soft hard body, feeling the pounding of her heart, made the world a place of order and sense.

It was a feeling which endured, miraculously, beyond taking her. I lay looking up at the sky and said, "You're the secular perfection of mankind."

After a long while she murmured, "Secular only?" "And divine." "Of mankind only?" "And of all beasts, birds and fishes." "Thank you, sir," she said.

We sang:

> *Wind of spring*
> *Please end the night*
> *And bring the rain—*

Not that it hadn't rained enough.

We came upon two large ponds, with the beginning of a path leading between them. The pines thinned out and we walked over dunes. Then we saw a large house, built in withered old stones and with over its door a tympanum on which Saint Benedict welcomed the weary traveler.

47

. . . .

THE SUPERIOR OF THE CISTERCIAN ABBEY OF CHAALIS WASN'T
too eager to follow the example of his patron saint.

He kept us waiting in a kind of anteroom the gatekeeper had shown us, a stone cubicle with a stone bench
in the middle and one porthole in the wall. We walked
around to keep warm for it was like a tomb there; then
we sat down huddled and with our arms around each
other. He finally found us like that and stared us up and
down, but I refused to be embarrassed; I looked at him
and did not remove my arm until he said: "I'm the superior of this abbey; did you ask for me?"

I stood up and said, "I'm Heron of Foix and, with her
permission, I'm presenting you Lady Claudia de Saint-
Jean."

"Yes?" he said.

"I've been trying to escort this lady to safety since her
house was destroyed. We're cousins," I added almost
automatically, for that was what we had always said before. "As you can see, we need rest and shelter."

The superior was a tall man; he must have been told

repeatedly that he had a classic profile and he now gave us a chance to admire it by gazing absent-mindedly out of the window hole. Then he turned and asked, "Which side are you two on?"

Claudia and I gaped; then we burst out laughing.

"I wasn't aware of being ridiculous," the monk said, reddening.

"Oh, to the contrary, Father," I managed to say. "We're just, er—rather weak with hunger. You asked a most Christian question."

The blush left his cheeks and gave way to pallor. "I'm in no need of instruction," he said. "I'll order some food brought to you here and then I'll beg you to be on your way."

"Oh dear, now you've done it," Claudia sighed when he had left, but she didn't really care.

An acolyte brought us bread, a piece of fish and a jug of water in which someone must once have dipped a dirty wineglass. I asked him what side his abbey was on in the fighting. He sighed; he looked like a peasant's son himself. "Ah, there's so many sides" was all I could get out of him. I handed him the gold coin I had been carrying and told him to go and show it to the father superior.

"We thank you for the meal," I said to the superior when he had re-emerged from the dark interior of that house, his face suspicious and amazed, holding the gold piece in his open palm, "and we want to make that a contribution to the abbey."

"You're mad," Claudia whispered behind me, but it worked: "You may stay and rest here awhile," he said dryly. "But the lady has to live in the outbuilding, I cannot allow her in the house. This is a place of asceticism."

Not for a moment had Claudia or I been angry or indignant at this man's manner. We were merely surprised: surprised that he still bothered so with the rules of the little game.

48
....

IN THE MORNING IT COST ME TWO BRIBES TO GET FIRST TO
the outbuilding (there was a passage from the refectory,
with a locked door), then out through the gate with
Claudia under a promise from the gatekeeper that we'd
be let back in.

We looked at each other; an old handyman living in
that place had repaired our clothes for both of us. "Did
you sleep well?" "Did you eat?" we asked. Then we were
silent, walking to the pond farthest from the house, cur-
ing ourselves from our separation of the night before. We
sat down in the sand.

Claudia put her arms around her knees and rested her
head on them, her hair shining against the yellow and
green around us. "You have a neck like the stalk of a
sunflower," I said, "and you've got blond streaks in your
hair."

"That's from our wandering. My father always made
me wear a headdress outdoors."

A silence.

With the rising sun the air and the ground became hot; we got up to walk around the pond and came to a place where its bottom showed sandy and without weeds. We took off our clothes and bathed; then we lay in the moving pattern of shade from a pine tree, stretched out hard on our backs and only her left hand touching my right hand.

We went back to the abbey just before sundown and had to separate, but I saw Claudia again at vespers—they had allowed her to attend with me, in the back of the chapel. There was a red, red sunset, painting the glass of the chapel's clerestory in the fiercest colors and bathing us all in a light of blood. The service passed as in a dream; I was aware of nothing but that garnet air enveloping Claudia and me.

Afterward we asked to see the superior again.

"We mean to ask you to marry us," I said.

He reflected. "I cannot," he answered. "I have no authority to marry cousins, not without specific permission of the Holy Father."

"Oh dear," Claudia said lightly.

I frowned. "Father," I said as solemnly as possible, "I must confess to you then that I have lied. We are not cousins."

He turned to leave the chapel; near the doorway he looked at me. "I didn't hear what you tried to tell me just now," he said, "if I had, I'd have to refuse you further shelter in this house."

We listened to the militant echo of his steps dying out in the corridor.

"What a wicked old man!" Claudia burst out.

"Oh, he isn't so bad. He thought he was being quite jolly; he almost winked at me just now when he left."

"He did?" she said, making her voice very high.

"Well, almost."

"How old are you, Heron?" she suddenly asked me.

"Nineteen."

"I hate everyone who is twenty or older," she said, "every single person in this world."

49
·······

AT SUPPER IN THE BARE REFECTORY I WAS IGNORED BY THE
monks, unable to leave the table until the endless prayers
had been uttered; and being away from Claudia now
hurt, in a simple and unsentimental way, like a thorn or
a bruise. But that night the arrival of a mendicant of the
order broke the silence in which the monks ate their
barley cakes and drank the thinned wine. The first thing
I realized from the talking was that Chaalis lay only a
few miles to the north of Ermenonville. Claudia and I
must have wandered in a wide arc.

The soldiers who had killed Robert were part of Navarre's men. Other French, and English, knights had
descended on Ile de France from all directions. The town
of Senlis, sheltering peasant soldiers just like Meaux, had
escaped the fate of that place and beaten off the attacking
nobles. Yet the massacres of Clermont and Meaux must
have broken the back of the people's rising. There had
been talk of having each village give up the four "most
guilty men" and pay a fine; but with the rising tide of

battle against the peasants that was forgotten and the knights wanted what they called total revenge.

The fighting on both sides was nothing more now than a monstrous trampling, as of a winegrower trying to kill a swarm of beetles invading his cellar. Neither knights nor peasants asked for side or name any more: everything standing in their paths was burned, every man run down. Name or money could no longer buy one's life. There was only death and counterdeath.

"What will be the fate of Chaalis?" the superior said aloud, as if asking that question of himself.

Paris was barricading itself, he was answered, and no other place offered any safety.

"God and Saint Benedict will protect us," came like a chant from the lower end of the table.

"God protects who protects himself," the superior answered thoughtfully.

I talked to the mendicant afterward. He was a young man, indescribably filthy—I could see the movement of the lice in his beard—but he was a scholar.

I told him how the superior had asked us which side we were on, and he smiled.

"You should have said, on the side of God," he said.

"I pray God's on my side. I'm on the side of man."

He asked me why I was there. Weren't there more important things than love right now, he said in a mocking voice. I asked, "Are there? If God doesn't make us all perish, it won't be for the sake of Charles of Navarre or

Edward of England. It might be for the sake of just two people loving."

He wasn't impressed with this thought.

He told me about the peasants he had seen entering Paris

50
. . . .

THERE IS A GIVING UP WHEN ALL SEEMS IN VAIN, BUT IT IS
no real giving up, for some untapped strength remains.
Such was the giving up in northern France in the spring
of that year, 1358, ten years after the great plague, two
years after the battle of Poitiers where the king was
taken and the defeated French knights became brigands.
It only took the very small miracle of Saint-Leu, nine
knights in mail slain by men in rags, to create an awaken-
ing. The serfs crawled out of their hiding places and,
watching the new portent, decided not that to desperate
men almost all is possible, but that their captive king
must have left England and somehow come to their aid.
They took up his battle cry "Montjoye," his banner with
the three golden lilies, and rose against their betters; and
they also started sowing the fields they had left bare. Sowing in late May: their humility toward the soil, which of
course disgusts a true gentleman, knows no bonds.

But now, in the final weeks of that rebellion, there was
a real giving up; that rare and almost mystical moment

had come when man had reached his limit. Knights who survived but whose companies were scattered didn't rebuild their houses but rode out of Ile de France and Picardy where no harvest would grow that summer. Peasants who survived abandoned the land and tramped toward Paris.

The monk had no idea how many had set out, how many had died. No one would ever know. He did say that if Ile de France had already seemed a desert to me some weeks earlier, it now looked like no landscape that was part of this earth. And the peasants who reached the city gates? They sat and lay in the streets and the squares, with their starving families clustering around them, with nowhere to go and no one who could do anything for them.

The only saint who seemed to bother with them was Saint Anthony, the monk said with a little smile, for the hogs of Saint Anthony which roam the streets of Paris now shared their rotten apples and plums, *nolens volens,* with the people of Ile de France who had escaped to that city.

51
· · · · · · ·

IT WAS A STILL, OVERCAST MORNING WHEN CLAUDIA AND I
came outside. The door to the outbuilding hadn't been
locked this time, and the gatekeeper had waved away
my customary little bribe. "They're afraid," I said, "and
so they've started worrying about their souls."

"Chaalis will burn too," Claudia said loudly and with
a core of satisfaction in her voice.

I stared at her; her face was so severe that it was like
someone else's. Then she caught my look, smiled at me
and was Claudia again.

We sat near our pond and she was cheerful, but I was
thinking about the mendicant. "Perhaps we should try
to reach Paris," I finally said to her.

Claudia jumped up. "Oh no!" she cried, "please not!
Promise me we won't."

"I can't bear the idea either," I began.

"I've put our fate in the hands of God," Claudia said
solemnly. "And in the hands of that Greek goddess. I
won't do any more running. I'm not going to have my-

self chased around like a rabbit by these men. I'm too proud!"

She looked fierce and very lovely.

"My father taught me," she said, "never try to outrun a thunderstorm. Find yourself a beech tree, and sit it out underneath. Well, you're my beech tree."

And I said to myself that indeed there was precious little to choose from, that the road to Paris would be as deadly as the abbey under attack by knights or peasants, that Claudia had no strength for more wandering, and that true chivalry would be to make my lady as happy as possible for as long as possible. And so I said, "I promise you, no more running."

When we came home that evening we saw from a distance that the gate was standing ajar. We quickened our step. The gate was open and the gatekeeper wasn't there.

We looked at each other with some consternation, and then I very cautiously went in. I walked softly down the corridor and inspected the refectory and some of the cells and finally the kitchens. Then I ran back to the gate to tell Claudia.

The abbey of Chaalis was standing empty. The monks had fled and only Saint Benedict knew exactly from what and where to.

52
. . . .

THE MOMENT WE HAD BOLTED THE DOOR BEHIND US, WE
both felt exhilarated. We stood in that grim hallway and
Claudia took my hands and said, "Let's do a little dance."
We dashed in and out of the rooms; the monks must
have left in a hurry for there was bread on the table,
chickens were loose in the courtyard and even books still
stood on their stands. Candlesticks, chalices, censers, the
golden Crucifix in the chapel, those things had gone.
"They've buried them somewhere, the crafty beggars,"
Claudia said. "More respect, girl," I told her.

"Think of it, Heron, we've got a whole abbey to ourselves. I'm a chatelaine again."

I bowed to her.

"Which room shall we take?" she asked.

We decided on the room of the father superior. It was
large and the warmest, facing south through a glass-
paneled window toward the pine trees which lined the
sand.

"But we don't want that silly bunk," Claudia said, kicking the ascetic bed of the superior.

"Certainly not."

I brought an axe from the kitchen and broke out the bunk. Then we dragged the thin mattresses and the covers from a whole row of cells to our room and built a beautiful bed. Darkness caught us unawares and we had to grope our way through the corridor to the chapel where we had seen candles.

Claudia knelt there; I stood silently beside her. And then she said quickly, "Will you Heron take me Claudia for your wife?"

I looked down upon her streaked hair, she didn't move, and I answered "Yes." She waited and so I knelt too and said, "And will you Claudia take me Heron for your husband?"

I choked a bit on those words, we sounded so pathetic.

"Yes," she answered. "In Nomine Patris et Filii et Spiritus Sancti."

"Et Aphroditae."

We lay in our bed and she asked, "Are you sorry you didn't go to England?"

"No," I answered.

Then I realized from her words that she knew as well as I did that I was no beech tree, and that there'd be no escaping. And each of us knew what the other was thinking, and we were strangely happy. We had stopped running from them, and we had our hour, "We've got the better of them," Claudia said; and "they" were: the old, the wicked, tired world.

She asked me, "Tell me about the sea? I've never seen it."

"It's a smooth glittering plain of water," I lied. "It looks just the way you see it in paintings."

In that room we had the early sun, rising at the very place where the trees stood thinner. It warmed the air and the stone walls, and we pushed the covers off the bed and lay as if we had entered paradise, but a paradise different from that of the University of Paris.

From far off a sound was heard of metal striking metal, of voices and horses' feet. Claudia sat up on her knees on the bed and peered through the window.

I felt under the mattress for my knife and just touched the handle, and quickly pulled my hand away before she'd notice what I was doing.

"I think they're coming," she whispered.

I put my arms around her hips and kissed her.

About the Author

Hans Koningsberger, now in his thirties, was born in Amsterdam, Holland. He served in the British Army during World War II, studied at the University of Zurich, and was a journalist and radio director in Europe and Indonesia. Much of his life has been spent in travel, but since 1951 this country has been his home, with New York and California his favorite states.

His previous novels, *The Affair* and *An American Romance,* were well received. He has won further praise for his translations of *The Ten Thousand Things* and *Yesterday* by Maria Dermoût, and has written a children's book and several plays.